A PATHWAY to MYSTERY

...and more

Contributors:

R.H. Burkett - DeDe Ramey - Shirley McCann
Ana Glenn - Art William L. Breach - James R. Wilder
Margarite Stever - J.C. Fields - Ken Gardner
Sharon Kizziah-Holmes - VJ Schultz - Lois Curran
Duane Laflin - Drew Thorn - Jen Kenning - Sage Hunter
Rosalie Lombardo - JJ Renek - Larissa Towers - Darcy Grace
Janet Kay Gallagher - Conetta Taylor - Nancy B. Dailey

Sleuths' Ink
Mystery Writers

2023 Anthology

A COLLECTION OF MYSTERY, SUSPENSE, THRILLER AND PARANORMAL
SHORT STORIES PENNED BY MEMBERS OF SLEUTHS' INK.

Edited by – Clarissa Willis
Cover Idea – Sleuths' Members
Cover Design – Ruth Hunter
Title – J.C. Fields
Publishing Coordinator – Sharon Kizziah-Holmes

Paperback-Press
an imprint of A & S Publishing
Paperback Press, LLC
Springfield, Missouri

ISBN -13: 978-1-960499-35-6

DEDICATION

In Memory of Nancy B. Dailey

 Nancy joined Sleuths' Ink after she and her daughter walked into a critique meeting almost 25 years ago. Having just lost her husband, she was looking for something to fill her time.

During the years she was a member, Nancy served as a Sleuths' Ink president, vice-president, treasurer, secretary, and was always willing to lend a hand when needed. She was a member of the Sleuths' JANO committee for the last few years and helped plan our annual JANO parties, where we award prizes to members for their writing accomplishments in the month of January.

In addition to being a writer, Nancy was also an established artist, having won many awards for her work over the years.

After a battle with ALS, our beloved friend passed away peacefully in her sleep on Monday, April 10th, 2023. Nancy never lost her spirit to live life to its fullest and she fought the disease with grace and dignity until the end.

CONTENTS

Dedication

ACKNOWLEDGMENTS

We are indebted to Dr. Clarissa Willis for the herculean task of editing these stories. She is an author, trainer, teacher, special educator, grant administrator, parent and member of Sleuths' Ink. We are lucky to have her talent counted among our ranks.

Sharon Kizziah-Holmes, owner and founder of Paperback Press guided the publishing process and lent her skills to the final formatting. We are lucky to count her as both a member, former board member of Sleuths' Ink and a friend.

Shirley McCann had the arduous task of gathering all the stories from all the writers and getting them prepared for the editor.

The cover design and title are a combination of ideas and images submitted by our members.

Finally, we would like to thank all the authors who submitted stories. Their enthusiasm and talents are what make this volume truly extraordinary for all of us here at Sleuths' Ink.

NOTE

Sleuths' Ink Mystery Writers is proud to bring you this amazing collection of forty-five short stories penned by our membership. We are a non-profit organization comprised of both seasoned authors and writers working toward this distinction. Many of our associates have multiple titles published and some will be able to point to this book as their first. No matter where our members are in their writing career, they all have a passion for the written word and telling a whopping good tale.

The 2023 Sleuths' Ink Mystery Writers Board of Directors

R.H. BURKETT

R.H. Burkett, aka Ruth Weeks, is an international tarot card reader who draws from her Cherokee and Cajun roots to write riveting tales of the paranormal. She currently lives in Springdale, Arkansas, with her familiar, Fred. Follow her at RHBurkett.com and on her author Facebook page where she shares tales and spells about the people she meets both from this world and the next.

NO BODY/NO CRIME

"Think she did it?"
  "Bet my badge on it."
  "Think we'll ever prove it?"
Detective Johnson shrugged. "What makes you think I want to? The guy was evil."
  "Not relevant. It's our duty to catch the bad guys."
  "Dani Mason is no bad guy."
  "True, never-the-less, I bet she did it."

Of course, I did it. Someone had to.
  At times the wheels of Justice move painfully slow. I just sped things up a little, that's all.
  Did I feel remorseful? Only if caught. That rat bastard beat the soup out of my best friend, killed her dog, and threatened her little boy. The creep deserved to die.
  "Earth to Dani."
  I shook loose from my thoughts. "Oh, sorry, Jeannie."
  "Trying to figure out who killed Tommy Whitmire? You know the police suspect a woman, don't you?"
  "Spit it out, Jean. You think I did it, don't you?"
  "Sorry. I was trying to be considerate."

"Not your forte, girlfriend."

"Did you? Kill him, I mean."

Now why would I admit to murder, especially to a nit-wit like Jeannie?

"Yes, Jeannie. I poisoned the guy, stabbed him ten times, shot him through the head, then buried him in a shallow grave so farmer Brown's dog could dig him up."

She laughed. "Okay. I surrender. Besides no one truly knows what happened. They can't find the body."

"Now, see? That's exactly why I don't understand any of this hoopla. Why do the cops even think a crime was committed? Maybe the rat scurried off to buy cheese or take a vacation in some garbage dump somewhere."

"The massive pool of blood found in his driveway might have something to do with it."

"Oh yeah, there is that."

Darn, it all. I knew I should've taken time to Clorox the cement. The only flaw in my plan. Well, not exactly. There was one detail that could prove problematic— his body was stuffed in my freezer.

"You're off the planet again, my friend. What is wrong with you?"

"It's not every day I have cops hauling me in for questioning, Jeannie. Excuse me if I'm a little scatterbrained."

"Dani, sometimes your sarcasm hurts. Everyone in this town knows you and Tommy had a checkered past."

"Checkered? He beat the stuffing out of my best friend. He would've done the same to her son if her Dalmatian didn't take a hunk out of his leg, which, by the way, he shot dead. I hated him."

"And that is why you're the main suspect."

"The jerk was a drunk. He sold crack to teenagers. Had a police record a block long. But I'm the one getting blamed for some phantom crime? Give me a break."

"No, give *me* a break. You made no bones about how

much you detested him. Shouted at the top of your lungs how if he ever touched Patty again, he'd be sorry."

"Never said I'd kill him."

"Oh, whatever. I'm out of here."

Jeannie thought she was my best friend. Not even close. My best bud was Patty Holiday.

Patty and I became best friends in the sixth grade when I told her how cool her last name was. From that day forward, we were joined at the hip. Patty was smart as a whip. Accelerated classes all through school. But for all her smarts, Patty had an Achilles' heel—men. More accurately, toxic men.

As so often happens, we lost track of one another when Patty went away to college. Fate, however, reunited us when she moved back years later with a baby. Deadbeat daddy split, never to be seen again. Lost and downtrodden, she knocked on my door one night and never left. We vowed always to have each other's back.

Neither Patty nor I ever dreamed how sadistic and mean her new boyfriend was until it was too late. Tommy used Patty like a punching bag more than once. It wasn't until he went after her little boy, that the crap hit the fan.

Damn straight I killed Tommy Whitmire.

I stopped and picked up Patty's pain pills before heading home. We had a job to do.

"Your mom come and pick up John Junior?"

"She just left."

"What did she say about your black eye and broken arm?"

"Kill the bastard."

Gotta love Mama Holiday.

"Dani? What did the cops say? They think you did it, don't they?"

"They asked a bunch of questions. I had answers for each one. They're fishing. No body, no crime. Right?"

"Right. Speaking of bodies. What are we going to do

with Popsicle Tommy?"

"I was rather hoping you had a solution."

"Well . . . actually I do have an idea, but it's far-fetched."

"Will it work?"

"One hundred percent."

"Then I don't care how crazy it is. Shoot."

"Bourbon first."

"You shouldn't drink with those pills."

"Oh, it's not me." Patti laughed.

This was going to be good.

"Hogs?"

"Yes. Virgil Ray told me a surefire way to get rid of a body is to throw it in a hog pen. They'll eat everything except the teeth."

"You talking about Virgil Ray, the old biker dude?"

"Yes. He was an MP in the army. He knows what he's talking about."

"Good enough for me. Where's the nearest hog farm?"

"Over the state line, about an hour from here."

"It'll be dark soon. Let's get Tommy loaded and ready to go."

"Oh . . . my . . . God. Dani? You didn't tell me you folded him in half!"

"He wouldn't fit in the freezer otherwise."

"He's a solid block of ice, weighs a ton. No way we can lift him out."

I searched my toolbox. Finally found a hammer and chisel. "This will work."

"Oh, sweet lord, you're not?"

"Got any better ideas? Bring that washtub over here."

I chiseled away at Tommy. Patty threw each piece into the tub. A foot here. A hand there. Each solid thud made both of us cringe. A few more shots of bourbon, and we were good to go. Patty helped me and, after a couple of tries, we finally got the tub into the trunk and slipped behind the wheel.

"You've been drinking. Better let me drive."

We both broke into hysterics. A DWI was the least of our worries.

The hog farm wasn't hard to find. We just followed our noses.

"Holy crap! Stinks worse than any chicken farm on earth."

Patty stood lookout. I threw each thawed-out piece of Tommy into the hog pen and watched the frenzy begin.

"Sooie pig!"

Patty broke the silence on the way back home.

"Dani? You know we'll go to hell for this."

"God forgives."

"You're a diabolical villain."

"Look me in the eye and tell me Tommy wouldn't have killed your innocent child?"

"I can't."

"Exactly. You think God wanted that?"

"No."

"We never speak of this again *ever*. Deal?

"Deal."

"Should we pull them over and arrest her now?"

Detective Johnson shook his head. "Nope."

"But, boss she just . . .

"Tommy Whitmire was the devil incarnate. Besides, no body, no crime. Case closed."

"But she did it."

Johnson smiled.

"Did what?"

DeDe Ramey

Born in central Texas, DeDe grew up with a very vivid imagination. She had a penchant for writing at a young age, writing lyrics, and skits, but didn't develop a desire to write romance novels until a few years ago. Once she let her imagination run wild, the dam broke, and all kinds of stories came to life. When she's not writing, she loves traveling with her husband, Keith and hanging out with her kids Drew and Allie, Corey and Leah, and her grandson Jude.

DeDe is a romance author with The Wild Rose Press. She writes the Dalton Skies series which includes- 24 to Life, *A Life Unknown, Life in the Limelight and Flashes of Life.*

BIG CITY LIFE

Iwas only there for a couple of days for an interview. When I booked my room, I scored a ritzy hotel with huge chandeliers and gold-plated accoutrements after researching some discount hotel hacks. My suite was on the twenty-seventh floor with a view of the skyscrapers and sparking lights of the city. I admit I was wowed and a bit proud of myself.

After dropping my bag off, I realized I hadn't eaten anything since breakfast. It was after seven, so I made my way down to the dining room. With the tables full and the noise setting my already frazzled nerves on edge, I opted for exploring what the city had to offer.

Checking the restaurants, I found a Greek deli that was just up the street. Perfect.

The sun was setting, and the clear blue sky was beginning to add shades of pink. I grabbed my coat, thinking it might be a bit chilly when I returned.

I stepped out the sliding doors to sirens filling the air. My attention was drawn up the street to a large man, dressed in the familiar blue uniform, unrolling a yellow crime scene tape. His cruiser, parked at the mouth of the alley, blocked most of the view, but I could still see someone lying on the pavement.

A dark scenario filled my mind recreating a story of what might have happened, and a sharp ache penetrated my chest as I wondered whose family member would not be returning home tonight. It was a horrible thought, but I figured this was probably a common occurrence in a big city like this. What a difference from my small-town life. Was this really the life I wanted?

A man, with a phone to his ear, bumped into me. His glare made me realize I hadn't moved. I turned and fell in step behind him, walking up the sidewalk filled with people. My mind drifted, wondering what their stories were, and where they were all going.

Checking my phone, it said the restaurant was another block away and when I looked up, I could see the sign. I continued behind the man from before, phone still to his ear, and was surprised when he ascended the stairs in the darkened alley that lead to the restaurant. As of yet, I hadn't heard him utter a word. Weird. Maybe he was listening to music. He was nicely dressed in a navy suit, but his hair was messy, like he'd run his fingers through it too many times. He grabbed the rail of the stairs and turned when he heard me behind him. My eyes searched his angry expression then landed on the stained cuff of the sleeve of his white shirt. I quickly lifted my eyes hoping he didn't notice. He didn't.

When I left the restaurant, he was still there, alone, staring out the window.

I told the police everything when I returned to the scene of the crime and figured it would bode well for my interview with the police department the next day to have already solved a crime.

EYE EYE CAPTAIN

"**N**o!" She screamed. Rob jerked, hearing the shrill sound. In town less than twenty-four hours and there was already something awry.

He turned to Ethan, his son, whose eyes had grown wide. "Get in the house and lock the doors," he instructed, then ran around the corner of the house wielding a large knife. The moving truck, in front of their small mid-century house, was still half full of items to be moved in. Rob squinted his eyes as he ran trying to figure out where the scream came from. His hat flew from his head, but he continued into the street stumbling off the curb.

A woman, with blonde wavy hair, was chasing a guy in a red sweatshirt. A black car sat in the middle of the road up ahead and Rob deemed it the getaway car. Racing past the woman he heard her scream, "He has my baby." Rob's chest tightened and he picked up speed. He had to catch the guy before he made it to the car, but if the guy was carrying the baby, how would he be able to tackle him without injuring the child?

Rob threw back to her, "Call nine-one-one." He didn't even want to get a glimpse of the woman's face. He couldn't imagine what she was going through or what he would do if someone grabbed Ethan.

The guy in the red hoodie glanced back. Rob could see him starting to fade, and he now appreciated all the endless practices running track in high school and college. Hearing the guy's footfalls, he knew he was nearly close enough. His arms pumped and legs strained. He had to get to him.

The roar of the car coming at them caught his attention. His hand flew up, reaching, barely grasping the guy's shoulder, spinning him around and pulling him down on top of him. The knife Rob held in his hand went flying in the process.

The hooded guy kicked and squirmed for release, but Rob tightened his hold. He hoped to hear the wail of a baby but there was nothing. Was the baby okay? Flipping the guy off him, he got his first glimpse of the assailant. A kid, no older than fifteen or sixteen. The bulge inside the zipped hoodie moved. Rob let out a relieved breath and sat on the kid's legs, quickly unzipping the hoodie only to find a fluffy honey-colored puppy. He grabbed it, and started to move off the kid, when his eyes caught the kid glancing at something over his shoulder. Rob knew someone had joined them. He quickly stood to his full height and spun around towering over another kid, about the same age, whose face paled when he realized what he was up against.

Out of the corner of his eye, Rob saw the hooded boy reach for the knife Rob dropped, and he couldn't help but chuckle. "What the...it's plastic."

Sirens pierced the quiet neighborhood. The hooded boy threw the knife down and the two thieves ran for the still-running car. Rob knew they wouldn't get far, and he had the pup nestled in his arms. His job was done. Reaching down, he picked up the knife, shoved it in his back pocket, and headed back up the street only glancing back when he heard the squeal of tires. "Busted," he sang.

Squinting ahead, he noticed the woman, with the wavy blonde hair, sitting on the step of her porch. She stood and ran when she saw him. "Oh my gosh, you saved him." The puppy squirmed and wiggled as she retrieved him from Rob's arms.

"The police are right behind me. They got the boys."

The woman glanced up at him with tears still streaking her face. "Thank you. I just got him a couple of weeks ago. I let him out for a second to go potty and the guy came out of nowhere."

Rob reached up and rubbed the soft fur of the puppy's head. "What's his name?"

"Milo."

Watching her golden curls float on the breeze, he realized just how pretty she was. "And yours?"

She blinked and a shadow of reluctance skimmed her face. "Oh, Kate." She paused, then held out her hand giving him a shy smile. Her eyes gazed past him. "I guess you're the new family moving in."

Rob glanced back over his shoulder as he took her hand. "Yeah. We were kind of taking a break when we heard you scream." He noticed broken down boxes by her garbage can. "I'm guessing you just moved in yourself?"

She followed his focus and nodded. "Oh, yeah. A couple of weeks ago."

"So, you moved *and* got a dog?"

"Yeah. You know, new place, all alone. I needed protection."

"Yeah, he looks like he could do some real harm." On cue, Milo barked. "Oh, sorry if I hurt your feelings."

"You didn't tell me your name."

Snapped out of his thoughts by her sweet voice, he responded, "Oh, it's Rob. Rob Baker."

"Well, thank you, Rob, for rescuing Milo."

"No problem." He turned to see the police car slowly pulling to a stop.

"Can I ask you something?"

His attention was dragged back to her with her question. "Sure, yeah, I guess."

"I hope I don't offend you by asking, but how'd you lose your eye?"

Confused he asked, "Come again?"

"Your eye." She pointed.

Rob reached up and felt the patch covering his left eye. He snickered then laughed. "I wondered why I felt a bit off balance when I was running." He jogged to his yard and retrieved the pirate hat and put it on. Yanking the plastic knife from his pocket, he stabbed it in the air. "My son found our Halloween costumes from last year in a box. I was Captain Hook, and he was Peter Pan. We were having a battle in the backyard when you screamed."

Kate laughed. He yanked the patch from his eye. Kate was even more beautiful through two eyes and Rob suddenly felt much better about his new location.

UNFORTUNATE MISUNDERSTANDING

"Yeah, go ahead and laugh," I said. "I bet it wouldn't be so funny if you had those shiny silver bracelets slapped on your wrists with the cops accusing you of stealing a million-dollar car." A snicker escaped as I stared at the most gorgeous man I had ever laid eyes on. Who, at the moment, sported a sheepish expression.

Nigel McDonough was that man; World-renowned architect turned GQ model and performance sports car aficionado. Who knew such a fine specimen of manliness, with such a big brain, could get embarrassed? But there he sat, across from me, in a small Austin deli, apologizing, again. I'll admit. It was kind of fun picking on him and watching his cheeks turn crimson.

His thick British accent was still laced with a bit of humor. "It was an unfortunate misunderstanding. I know buying you a sandwich will not make up for it. But maybe it could be a start."

Misunderstanding is an understatement. More like a miscommunication. It started with a phone call a few weeks ago from Donny Mullins, the coordinator of the Texas Tuff Charity Race. He told me the driver for Mr. McDonough's Ferrari had bowed out and asked if I would be interested.

Of course, I was interested. This race was turning into a well-known yearly event with high-performance racers from all over the United States. I have wanted to race in this competition since it started, and to get a chance to race one of Nigel McDonough's cars was the icing on the cake.

I was instructed to pick up the Ferrari at Mr. McDonough's garage. It was early; five A.M. I entered the code I was given, and when the door opened, the lights automatically came on. Before me were at least a dozen high-performance sports cars from Lamborghinis to Porches to McLarens, Lotus' and even a Bugatti. You name it, he had at least one, and each was worth at least a million dollars.

I hit the key fob and lights flashed on a deep ruby-red Ferrari. If I could choose one car to race in the whole wide world, it would be this Ferrari. I climbed in, took a deep breath and started the engine. I paused for a moment to let my heart settle, then headed to the exit. About halfway to the door, I heard an alarm. Not thinking anything of it, because I was doing everything I was told, I continued, but called Donny to let him know. He didn't pick up, so I left a message.

The racers driving from Dallas coordinated to leave from Apex Industries parking lot. There were almost a hundred of us. We decided to have some fun and wagered who would make it to Austin first. Though I wasn't the only woman in the race, I was the youngest and a rookie, so I had something to prove.

Outside of Austin I stopped at one of the drive-thru restaurants to grab something to eat since I was close to the front of the pack. McDonough didn't spare a dime on his cars. They were the best of the best, and fast. Oh, so fast. I pulled onto the highway and hit the gas to regain my lead and suddenly, there were red and blue strobes in my rearview mirror. Dammit! I had never been pulled over.

The officer walked up to my window and I smiled. He

looked surprised, then he recited his usual stupid question of, *"Do you know how fast you were going?"*

He was nice enough looking, so I debated about flirting with him. Since he busted my chances of winning the wager, I figured it wouldn't hurt and said, "About one twenty-five the last time I looked." Then, gave him my best sultry smile.

He then asked, "Was there a reason why you were speeding?"

I couldn't help myself. I said, "Well, yeah. I didn't want my fries to get cold." I picked up the bag. "Want one?" He actually laughed and took two. I seriously thought I got him, and he was going to let me off. They had a few of us pulled over in different spots so they couldn't very well haul us all in.

"Are you part of the group we've been trying to pull over?"

"Yeah." I wasn't going to lie. "There's over a hundred of us coming from Dallas, heading to the Circuits of America for the Texas Tuff Charity Race." He laughed, then let out a long breath looking at the handful of cars that were pulled over.

But then I heard the dispatcher on the radio say the car had been reported stolen. "Stolen? Oh, hell no." The officer's smile disappeared. I tried to tell him my story, but before I knew it, the handcuffs were around my wrists, and I was being escorted to the backseat of his cruiser. I was so pissed I couldn't see straight. Gone were my chances of racing at the Circuit of America and my hot fries. I am going to kill whoever dropped the ball on this.

I called Donny and quickly found out who needed to be killed. He said he forgot to tell me about keying in the anti-theft code on the car. The next thing I knew, Nigel McDonough was bailing me out and rushing me to his car. "I'm sorry for the misunderstanding," he said yanking open the door. "I'm going to try to get you to the track in time for you to race."

"I'm sorry for the trouble."

"Not your fault, love. It wouldn't have happened if Donny would have told me Alex Scott was a girl." We headed to the track, found my team, and I suited up.

I didn't win, but I got into the money which was a freaking miracle with how everything unfolded. They know who Alex Scott is now, and it's not just Max Scott, the five-time Tread Master champion's granddaughter.

Who knew an unfortunate misunderstanding could lead to the best day of my life?

DEAD RINGER

The black sedan slammed on its brakes. Krissy screamed and threw up her hands, bracing for impact as the car's horn blared. She slumped when the car skidded to a stop, inches from hitting her. Her eyes connected with the man behind the wheel, and she gave him an 'I'm so sorry' smile then whipped her head around searching for the ghost she'd seen, but he was gone. It was him.

Slowly she turned and continued her walk toward the coffee shop; her heart still racing; her eyes still searching. She vaguely heard the profanities being tossed at her by the irate driver, but it didn't register. All she could think about was him. He was alive and in New York. How did he find her? They told her she was safe.

She had uprooted her entire life to go into hiding because of him, and now he knew exactly where she was. He saw her. She nearly walked right into him. Was he watching her? She stopped abruptly, and a woman bumped into her. She apologized, but the woman barely regarded her. That was New York City. She didn't think she would ever get used to it. There were so many people, and everyone moved so fast. So how did he find her amongst the massive population? It would be impossible. And what

19

now?

Her plans had been to grab a coffee and head to the art gallery just like every other day for the past few months. But now, thoughts of what seeing him meant were racing through her brain. She needed to call her contact. Needed to quit her job. Needed to go back into hiding because there was no way he wouldn't come after her and probably kill her.

But why did he react so oddly when he saw her? Although she had changed her hair, she didn't look that different than when they dated. But he acted confused like he almost didn't even recognize her. Was it because she was out of her normal element? He'd come looking for her. Right?

It didn't matter. What mattered was what came next. She scanned her surroundings, then peered into the picture window of the coffee shop, and not seeing anyone resembling him, she tugged open the door. Nothing could be accomplished without coffee.

After taking a few sips of the bitter liquid, she retrieved her phone and called a familiar number. "Renfro."

At the sound of his voice, a lump formed in her throat, and she wasn't sure she was going to be able to speak around the emotion that had collected. "You lied to me."

"Who is this?" he questioned with an audible huff.

"It's Krissy Wolf. You lied."

"Lied about what?"

"Devin."

"What about Devin?"

"He's not dead. He's very much alive and he's in New York City."

"Trust me Krissy, he's dead. I don't know who you saw, but it wasn't Devin McAlester. And even if it was, it's highly unlikely he found you."

"I'm telling you, it's him, and he's here."

"Krissy, it's not him. I'm the one who found him. He

killed himself." She stopped at a crosswalk while she waited for the signal to change, unable to get the vision of Devin out of her head.

At one time, she had been completely in love with the man. His easy smile and twinkling blue eyes always told her he was up to something and kept her heart captive until she realized he wasn't who he claimed to be. He said he was an architect from Albuquerque, New Mexico who had been hired by a California technology company to design a new state-of-the-art headquarters that was going in on the outskirts of her little town of Peyton. She'd met him when he first came to look at the location, and their relationship blossomed with each of his return visits.

He constantly held her and kissed her like he couldn't get enough of her. They loved with an intensity she had never experienced before. He said she was his life source and felt like he was dying every time he had to return to Albuquerque. She had started putting in applications at art galleries in Albuquerque, preparing to move her life there to be with him.

She'd bought his story hook, line and sinker until she happened to see a Crime Stoppers story about a young girl who had been murdered a few towns away. The story showed a blurry image captured by a nearby camera of a person of interest. Krissy noticed a resemblance to him but brushed it off. He would never do anything like that. He was too sweet. Then she lost her keys while visiting him in Albuquerque. While searching his car, she unlatched his console and within the compartment were items that left no question as to who he really was. A cold-blooded killer. From that moment her life as she knew it was no more.

Before his case went to trial, though, he disappeared. Krissy was taken to a safe house, where she stayed until word came that they'd found him dead. She breathed a sigh of relief. Until today.

No matter what Craig Renfro told her, she knew the man

she saw was Devin. She picked up the pace as she closed in on the gallery. A hand gripped her shoulder and she jerked. "Krissy?"

Slowly she turned and made eye contact with a familiar face. Her stomach dropped. "But they said you died," she whimpered as tears pooled in her lashes.

"Devin did die. I'm Colin." He smiled, but she could see something evil within his eyes.

Studying his face for a long moment, she jerked away from him. "Don't pull that crap on me, Devin." She took a step away from him. "Stay away from me."

"We're twins." Somewhere in the back of her mind, she remembered Devin saying he had a brother he'd lost contact with, but never said they were identical twins. "It has taken me forever to find you."

"How did you find me? And why?"

"Let's just say I'm resourceful. Money speaks volumes. And why? Well, being a twin has its perks. They can take the fall for you when you unexpectedly get in trouble. Even better when their girlfriend throws them under the bus. Woohoo. Good job," he said releasing a sinister chuckle. "But unfortunately, you, my lovely Krissy, are still a loose end."

STOLEN MOMENTS

I pushed at the door, and it opened. Surprise. The lights were off, but the streetlamps lent me enough light to see the merchandise inside. I shook off the water from my jacket and quietly proceeded inside, still astonished that the store wasn't locked up tight. Someone's forgetfulness is my good luck. Looking around, the place was filled with high-end electronics, worth tens of thousands of dollars.

As I examined the offerings, a noise pulled my attention to the back of the store and the silhouette of a woman appeared in the doorway. She jumped when she saw me and let out an ear-piercing scream.

Her hand flew to her chest. "Oh, my gosh, you scared me. We, we won't be open for—" her voice sent a shiver through me. She closed the distance between us, and her features were illuminated by the light outside. Chestnut hair was pulled into a high ponytail. Sapphire blue eyes were wrapped with thick dark lashes, and her scarlet-colored lips practically beckoned me to taste them. I could nearly taste their sweet flavor. Even though she was dressed in a plain black long-sleeved T-shirt and dark jeans, everything hugged her curves perfectly and left nothing to my imagination. The girl I fantasize about every night was standing in front of me and she was more stunning than I could ever imagine.

The way she was studying me momentarily caused me to lose my focus on why I was there. I stumbled for a moment, wondering if there was a way to escape, but not really wanting to. My eyes tracked up her body to her face and I decided to take my chances. "I'm so sorry." I turned and motioned to the door. "I noticed your door was open and—"

"You're here to fix the leak, aren't you? My dad told me he called someone, but I wasn't expecting anyone until later this morning."

"What? Oh, yes. The leak. I thought I would try to come in before the store opened and you had customers. I was surprised when I saw the door..." My concentration was shot with the way she looked at me. I wasn't even sure she bought my load of crap, but I continued. "Also, with the way it's raining, I can gauge how bad the leak might be."

"Good idea. Let me show you where it's at. Follow me." She turned and I ran my fingers through my wet hair as I followed behind her watching her brown curls sway across her back. "My name is Sadie, by the way," she said, turning to glance at me. "You're Troy, right?"

I was so mesmerized by the way her body moved that I forgot to answer, again. She turned and her eyes cut to me looking a bit concerned. "Oh, yes, Troy. Sorry. I was checking out the ceiling for possible stains from leaks," I lied.

"Oh. Okay." She continued her trek through shelves of extra stock until we took an abrupt turn, and she flipped on the light and pointed. "There."

A five-gallon bucket sat in the corner of what looked to be the employee lounge area. It was sparsely furnished with a small table and chairs, a refrigerator, and an old couch that took up most of one wall. The bucket was about half full of dirty water and, from the looks of the leak, it wouldn't be long before it was full. I looked around for a moment then suddenly felt her hand on my shoulder and spun around to see those beautiful blue eyes flickering with a smoldering flame.

"Do you think you can handle it?"

The tone in her voice told me she wasn't talking about the leak. I couldn't help but smirk. I'd seen and done quite a bit in my life, but this, this was a first. When in Rome, though...

"Oh, yeah, I can handle it." The smoldering flame in her eyes exploded into a raging firestorm and her fingers traced a trail down my arm leaving stings of electricity in their wake. I stepped forward, taking a chance. She didn't move. This was going to be fun.

Leaning forward, I kept my gaze locked on her for a reaction. The tip of her tongue wet her plump bottom lip and I knew, in that moment, I was golden. My eyes flicked to the old couch at the edge of the room, and I wondered what might happen on it in the next few minutes, then I felt her lips on mine. Surprised at her boldness, I flinched, but then snaked my arm around her and pulled her into me. Wrapping my hand behind her head, I nestled my fingers in her bourbon-colored locks. I knew it was so wrong, so stupid, so careless and dangerous, but in the moment, it felt absolutely right.

Her hands pushed up over my shoulders at my heavy jacket. It hit the floor with a clang and my heart stopped. Her eyes tipped up to mine as her lips pulled away just enough for me to say, "Tools." That's all she needed for her lips to find mine again as her fingers started to unbutton my worn button-down. I tightened my grasp around her waist and pushed her over to the couch, slowly lowering her down. Trailing kisses down her neck, I let her continue to remove my shirt and then my T-shirt. Was this seriously happening? Delicate hands traced around the muscles of my chest making my body ignite.

I pulled off her long-sleeved shirt, finding a soft yellow

T-shirt that read 'sunshine with a little hurricane' and chuckled at how fitting it was for her. She lit me up like a noonday sun and set off a hurricane of emotions that I was not prepared for. Getting away with petty crimes had always been my adrenaline fix, but in a matter of minutes, this goddess had me willing to give it all up to be able to have a life with her.

I let my fingers skid under the hem of her shirt and explored the silky skin of her belly, then pushed it up and dropped wet kisses up the center of her stomach to her breast. Rubbing the pad of my thumb over her lace-covered breast, she sucked in a breath and my eyes met hers, making sure she was not second-guessing our little rendezvous. Her teeth skated across her bottom lip and there was that smirk again. Oh yeah, she was good with it. My hand slipped behind her and unclasped her bra, and with the release of her perfect, delicate breasts, my control snapped. I was desperate to have her.

My mouth found hers again and her hands pulled at my belt. Our bodies collided as we tugged at each other's remaining clothes. My heart pounded erratically, and my eyes connected one last time before we stepped across the threshold of no return. Uncertainty flashed across her flushed face, and I paused. "Are you sure you're—" I drew out the question studying her expression, and she interrupted before I was able to finish.

"Absolutely." Her fingers threaded through my damp hair. "I mean, I've never done anything so reckless. My dad—"

I cut her off, trying to keep her brain from steering off course, from possibly getting suspicious about me. Pulling her beneath me, she slowly lifted her eyes to me and suddenly I was lost. Who was getting steered off course? What was I here for exactly? Everything around me was out of focus except her staring up at me, and I've never felt more whole in my life. I'd been a petty thief for most of my life, seeking out that adrenaline rush, but this far surpassed anything I had ever felt, and we hadn't done anything.

My body trembled, craving her, needing to claim her. Slowly lowering my body against hers, I took her mouth in a tender kiss, suddenly wanting this to be much more than a random hook-up. Her tongue brushed against mine as I skimmed her skin with my fingertips making my way to her hip. Then pulling her against me I pushed into her center and with the sound of her soft whimper, life, as I knew it, disappeared. I knew in that instance she was all I would ever need. I vowed in that moment to never steal anything again if only I could keep her forever. She was my perfect high.

Her fingers dug into my back, as her gasps turned into moans, and I knew I was moments away from ecstasy.

Staring at her beautiful face, her lips parted dragging in a gasp. Her eyes opened wide, back arched, and she let out a cry as her body spasmed with her release taking me with her.

Our bodies were slick with sweat as we tried to steady our breaths. I raised up and moved some wayward hair from her face. She scraped her teeth across her bottom lip then the corner of her mouth tipped up. I battled against smiling back but I lost miserably because, even though I barely knew the woman, she had made me happier than I had been in a long time. And I was hoping she would be open to continuing to make me happy. She lifted up just enough to place soft kisses along my neck and I got the feeling I might have a chance. The chime of her phone interrupted us. With a deep breath, she backed away, and my body immediately begged for more. She put one finger up asking me to wait while she pulled her phone from the pocket of her jeans laying on the floor.

"Hey dad, what's up?" Her eyes darted to mine and a half-smile curled on her lips. "Okay. I think I have things handled, but thanks for letting me know." A smirk crossed her face as she disconnected the call.

"What's that look on your face for?"

"My dad was telling me he got a call from the guy coming to fix the roof. Apparently, he's going to wait out the storm."

I stiffened and sat up, knowing the jig was up. Dread washed over me as I watched her return her phone to her pants pocket, knowing that her next comment would probably be, *"get out."* I should have known this would happen. Should have seen it coming. Hell, I deserved it. But the minute I looked deep into her eyes, I knew I wanted to spend the rest of my life with her.

She tucked a strand of hair behind her ear and looked up at me as she slowly sat up. A playful gleam filled her eyes, confusing the hell out of me. Her fingers threaded through my hair and her breath brushed against my cheek as she spoke. "Relax. I knew. I saw you casing the place a few days ago. I immediately recognized you when I saw you this morning and figured I caught you in the act, so I thought I would have some fun. Heck, with the sound that came from your jacket earlier, you had already pocketed some stuff. You're quick!"

I couldn't help but chuckle. "So, you knew the whole time?"

She nodded and giggled. "The roofer's name is Dan. He's an old friend of my father's. Probably in his sixties." I shook my head and let out a belly laugh. She had me. "But ask me if I care." Her hand wrapped around my neck and pulled me into her, kissing me once again.

"I may have just stolen something after all."

SHIRLEY MCCANN

Shirley McCann's fiction has appeared in Woman's World, Alfred Hitchcock Mystery Magazine, and The Forensic Examiner. She lives in Springfield, Missouri, where she loves spending time with her friends and family.

CHEERS

"**D**ave, get over here. You're never gonna believe this."

Dave sauntered over to his friend, Mark. "You're probably right. I'm never going to believe it. Because every time you think you've made a momentous discovery, it turns out to be nothing."

"Not this time, my friend. This one will make us millions. Maybe even billions."

Dave blew out a breath and crossed his arms. "Okay, what am I looking at?"

"I can bring a dead person back to life."

Dave laughed out loud. "You have really gone off the deep end this time."

Mark felt his friend's hand on his shoulder, but he shrugged it off. "I knew you wouldn't believe me. You continually rain on my parade. No matter what idea I come up with, you're always the first to poo poo the idea." He heard another heavy sigh as Dave took a seat next to him at the large table. "I gotta be honest. Your constant skepticism is starting to grate on my nerves."

He heard fingers tapping on the table and knew his friend was getting annoyed. But if Dave left now, the whole plan would go up in smoke.

"Mark, you have to realize this idea is preposterous. Once a person is dead, there is no way they can come back to life," Dave said.

He leaned across the table and put a hand over his friend's to stop the annoying tapping. Mark needed the man's cooperation. But before he could say anything, Dave spoke up.

"Look, I admit, I've been less than supportive of your inventions so far, but you have to know, my friend, that this ridiculous idea puts you way outside the realm of reality."

Mark offered a placating smile. "Just hear me out," he said. "Can you just listen with an open mind for once?"

Dave smiled and nodded. "Okay, I'll listen. But I hope you've got something to drink around here, 'cause I'm gonna need something really strong to keep an open mind for this crazy notion."

Minutes later, Mark appeared with a bottle of scotch and a tumbler of ice. "Enjoy while I explain how this works. I promise you won't be disappointed."

Dave opened the bottle and poured himself a generous amount then took a long slow sip. "Just keep the scotch coming, and I'm all yours." He took another sip, then said, "By the way, how are you gonna prove your theory anyway? You don't have a dead body lying around here, do you?" His sarcasm was grating on Mark's nerves, but he kept his cool.

Mark smiled. "Of course not. I just want to explain to you how this works, and then we'll test it out. Maybe we can pick up a homeless person somewhere later to test the actual theory on. No one would miss him."

Dave rolled his eyes but continued with his drink. When his glass was empty, he grabbed for a refill.

"Okay, here's how this works." Mark stood up and walked across the room to where he'd set up a table with various bottles of liquid.

"I'm all ears," Dave said, his words a bit slurred. Mark's

grin widened. This was going so well. He picked up a bottle of the blue liquid and brought it over to where his friend had almost devoured an entire bottle of scotch. His head hung low toward the table, and his glassy eyes appeared vacant as he cradled an almost empty glass.

Mark slammed the bottle on the table to get Dave's attention. "You see this bottle?" he said. Dave nodded, although Mark was pretty sure the man's mind had already left the room "This bottle contains a special concoction that will, in theory, bring a dead person back to life."

"Sure..., sure..., sure..." His words were slow and slurred.

Mark picked up the bottle and opened the lid. "You're gonna be the first one to try it," he told his friend.

Dave laughed, at least, it sounded like a laugh. The man was so drunk now, he probably couldn't stand if he tried.

"One problem," he mumbled. "I'm not dead."

Mark sat down across from him. "You will be. That scotch is full of poison."

"Wha...?" His eyes widened in horror moments before his head crashed onto the table.

Mark got up, walked around the table and poured the blue liquid down the man's throat. When nothing happened, he smiled and said, "Guess you were right, Dave. Dang stuff doesn't work."

LILY'S DILEMMA

L ily Baker stopped to catch her breath, while her trembling fingers gripped the door of the coffeeshop she and Jane often frequented.

Tears streaked down her face. She rubbed her eyes, noticing the black from her mascara staining her hands.

"Oh Jane," she whimpered, as the image of her friend's bloodied body, lying at an odd angle on their living room floor, flitted through her mind. Her scream echoed off the walls when she noticed the dark-clothed man walking toward her, the glint of a knife's long silver blade clutched in his hand.

With each step he took, an eerie tune of danger echoed in her ears. Fear gripped her heart, and she'd turned and ran out the door.

Pulling herself to a standing position, she turned the knob to the coffee shop, surprised it opened. Jerry closed the shop at ten PM sharp, so why was it open now at midnight?

She didn't have time to think about what that might mean. If she didn't hide, she was as good as dead.

She lunged inside and turned the lock, securing herself from the maniac who searched for her. Sliding to the floor, she breathed a sigh of relief then realized she could still be seen from the glass door.

Crawling across the room, she hugged her knees against the bar, then allowed herself to call out softly. "Jerry? Are you here?"

Her eyes finally adjusted to the darkness, and she dared a peek outside, relieved to see no one there.

"Where are you, Jerry?" she said a bit louder.

She stood up and fumbled her way across the room, calling out the owner's name as she went. From previous visits she knew there was a telephone behind the bar. She swallowed hard fumbling her way until she found it. Breathing a sigh of relief, she picked up the receiver and punched in 911.

No dial tone.

"Jerry!" Frustrated, she screamed his name louder. He had to be here somewhere. No way would he go off and leave the front door unlocked.

But why no dial tone?

Her breathing quickened, and she felt faint. She gulped deep breaths of air, feeling the fear suffocating her like a vise around her chest.

The loft, she thought. Jerry must be in the loft apartment. He'd probably just forgotten to lock the door.

She crept toward the back door and out into the alley calling out his name softly. "Jerry, are you here?"

The serial killer that roamed the streets of town had already killed her best friend and was now after her. She needed the police, but with no way to call for help, Jerry was her only hope. Lily refused to be another victim.

She turned the corner and put her hand on the railing leading to Jerry's loft when her heart caught in her throat. The man in black stopped his ascent up the stairs and turned to face her.

"Welcome, Lily," Jerry said. "I knew you'd show up here."

ANA GLENN

Ana Glenn began her award-winning mystery writing after joining Sleuths' Ink a few years ago. Before that, she expressed her thoughts through poetry. She was born in Southwest Missouri and has lived in California, Texas, and settled home again in Missouri. In 2014, after 42 years, two children, and three grandsons, she was widowed. She reconnected with her childhood sweetheart in 2020. She retired in 2021 from an Automotive dealership accounting and dealership consulting career to devote time to her family and the two (soon to be 3) great-grandchildren. She is working on a family history, two mystery novels, and compiling her poems into a book.

PATH TO RAGE

It was a crisp October evening when I pulled into our hidden driveway. I was anticipating his joy and surprise as I arrived a day early. I didn't recognize the strange vehicle parked in the first opening in the evergreens lining our drive. Partially hidden in the trees, the Jeep taillights reflected my headlights. I turned off my lights and pulled into the next clearing. I headed up the drive to our home with the Glock I always carried drawn. I wasn't sure what I'd encounter, but I was unprepared and shocked by the scene unfolding on my front deck. There in the moonlight were the intimately intertwined shadows of my husband of three years and, judging by the hairstyle- Rachel, one of the women who, as my professed friend, constantly chastised me for my fearlessness and free spirit. Ironic; my bravery and soul were among the many traits Joseph always told me he loved and admired.

My mind was racing, as well as my heart. Should I confront the cheaters or leave and say nothing? I quietly ran back to my Lexus LX to think or attempt to. My mind kept screaming, "Liars, Adulterers, I want you gone from my home!" After all, it was my home legally. It was in the prenup Joseph insisted we write up, so his assets remained his, and mine were mine. After his divorce, he was always afraid someone would take what he'd worked hard to get. As I slumped in the leather seats, I remembered the cameras we had installed and attempted to access them on my phone. They were offline - no surprise. Joseph prided himself on his cleverness and would leave no evidence of his adultery. His infidelity and complete dismissal of the vows we exchanged infuriated me. I am enraged and seeing red by now- blood red- his and hers!

I've never been violent, and betrayal is a product of a long life. I always managed to bury my anger and move on with my life. No more- I would tell them what I thought! I threw open my car door and ran up the path, sobbing as if my heart would break. They were still intertwined and didn't hear or see me until I chambered a round. The look on both of their faces was priceless. Strangely, neither of them attempted to cover their nakedness or speak. They just stared at my hand and their potential death. I saw them for their pure evil, and my only thought was justice is required- justice for their betrayal of me, our marriages, friendship, and the hundreds of imperfect lives their judgmental tongue wagging has ruined. I pulled the trigger twice and watched as the lifeblood drained from their cold hearts. I dialed 911 to confess my evil deed.

THUNDER AND LIGHTNING
ROLL AGAIN

The clap of thunder awakened me from another night of fitful sleep.

My bedroom's suddenly as bright as day with the brilliant flash of lightning and another crack of thunder. Startled awake, and I'm still groggy from the Four Roses I drank to give into slumber earlier.

Garth Brooks is playing on the radio, and the song lyrics become clear. "And the thunder rolls, and the lightning strikes, another love grows cold on a sleepless night."

I flashback to the time my life mirrored a Garth Brooks song. It was 1978, and I was a young wife and mother of a two-year-old precious little girl. I'd just found out I would have our second child. My husband was out with his best friend, Steve, helping him through the first few nights of his latest breakup. Steve was such a nice guy, so it was hard to figure out why women always broke his heart. Dave was helping him through another night beer drinking and cruising Belmont Avenue, the main drag in town where mostly high school kids hung out. High school kids and not-so-young men trying to regain the freedom and carefree times of their youth. A time before Vietnam, wives and families shattered their carefree days—a time when they didn't stare into the faces of their loving family and see only responsibilities. A time the memories of war didn't awaken them in a cold sweat while fighting an enemy only they could see.

That night was like many others, left at home alone because it wasn't safe, or it was too hot or too cold for me to go along. He worried about my health, especially with our much-wanted and planned-for baby on the way. We couldn't afford a babysitter, and he didn't want his parents to watch our precious girl all night, so I stayed home again with our little one.

That night more than most I had a sick feeling that something wasn't right. I attributed it to the all-day morning sickness this pregnancy brought. Dave showered and changed out of his regular work clothes tonight because it was so hot and humid. A cool shower would refresh him after a long day of work. Being a gullible and totally in love young woman, I believed him because the alternative was too painful to entertain.

My precious Cheri and I played for a few hours until she fell asleep on her favorite stuffed bear. After I carried her to bed, I fell asleep on the sofa waiting for David to get home. Just like tonight, I was jolted from a fitful sleep by the clap of thunder, followed closely by the bright flash of lightning filling the room. I hurried to Cheri's room to find her peacefully sleeping like a little angel.

Again, I had that sick feeling in the pit of my stomach, not morning sickness but a sense of something being terribly wrong. The overwhelming feeling that I must head to Belmont Avenue to look for David was too strong to ignore. I gently lifted Cheri and placed her in her car seat for the late-night trip downtown. I'd only been there once when David drove me there and showed me his favorite high school Saturday night route.

As I rounded the corner onto Belmont, I spotted David's

custom truck at his favorite convenience store. Steve was standing by the passenger door kissing a dark-haired woman, and David was standing next to the driver's door holding a blonde woman in his arms. As I pulled into the parking lot, my lights shone directly on them, and they looked in my direction. Instantly, they jumped into the truck and headed out the side street driveway with the truck lights out. As I made my way across the parking lot, I could see the two women clearly and recognized the blonde who was a customer at David's body shop earlier in the week. I headed in the direction I thought he had traveled, but I couldn't be sure because I had no taillights to follow. I never did catch up to them. Even with a strong V-8, I was no match for his big block custom Chevy high-performance engine. I drove home after driving by Steve's apartment to find they hadn't returned there. Shaking from betrayal, hurt and anger, I tucked Cheri in her bed and returned to the darkened living room to wait.

It was approaching dawn when I heard the truck round the corner and shut the engine off to coast into the driveway. I watched out the window as David used a shop rag to wipe his face and neck before heading to the door.

He was surprised when I opened the door before he could put his key in the lock and asked, "What are you doing up so late?"

"Don't you mean so early?" I replied.

"What?" he bellowed, "it's still the middle of the night."

"Why did you run when you spotted my car on Belmont tonight, and who was that woman you were with?" I yelled.

"What the hell are you talking about? You're crazy."

"I know what I saw, and you left the parking lot with your lights off! I saw you and Steve and those two women you were with!"

I never even saw him raise his fist, but I felt the excruciating impact on my jaw. The impact knocked me to the sofa. Thankfully, I don't remember every blow but when I woke up, David was passed out in bed. I checked my unrecognizable image in the bedroom mirror and went to phone the police. It took forever to find the number in the phone book- this was pre-911. I had no difficulty in giving my address and details to the officer. Even in 1978, a beating with the evidence on my face elicited charges.

Pregnant and with a toddler, I was about to embark on a long, frightening journey.

THE FINAL STORM

◆ ◄◄ ◆ ►► ◆

That last thunderclap shakes both floors of this old farmhouse. The thunderstorm is getting closer and more severe by the minute. Flashes of lightning turn my bedroom as bright as the sunniest summer day. I can hear the hail pelting against my windows. I used to love these early spring storms- before I had to face them alone. Sam always made me feel safe in his strong arms on our porch swing as we marveled at their beauty and fury.

Back to reality, I'll have power from my new generator and not be totally in the dark. So glad installation was before tornado season begins here in Missouri. I was fortunate not to lose power during the recent ice storms that destroyed the old oak tree where we sat and watched our squirrel family throw acorns at us. I feel close to Sam, remembering how they came closer daily and eventually ate chocolate chip cookies from our laps. Tonight, I plan to curl up with the dog-eared Country Living magazine we used as our guide to turn this into our "Heaven on Earth." Strange how our dream has become my nightmare and my private hell.

Since Sam's disappearance, I've thrown myself into finishing this 1800's farmhouse and land we bought three months before that fateful day. It was our dream to retire early and turn it into our dream home. It's hard to believe it's been two years since he went for supplies and never was seen again. There are no charges on his credit cards since that fateful day. I was the last person to see him, so the sheriff said I was their prime and only suspect. It was devastating to lose my love of twenty-seven years. The suspicion that I was responsible for his disappearance only increased my pain. The two-million-dollar life insurance policy we purchased two years before we moved is the suspected reason I killed him.

We were new to the area, and the cloud of suspicion over my head weighed heavily on my heart and reputation. I heard the whispers. "She may look tiny and weak, but she did away with her big, strong husband. I'm truly alone here. Our family lives a world away in California. Covid restrictions made it impossible for them to help me search and investigate his disappearance. I've searched every possible route asking everyone if they saw him or his truck the day he disappeared. The answer was always no.

I can't let my heart believe he's gone. I still feel his presence. Our families tell me to petition to have him declared dead. He was and is my life. I can't give up yet. I've checked every file on his computer, although Deputy Stark and his computer forensic experts found nothing useful. He's the one person who has tried to help me in my quest for Sam. I'm looking for any clue about what happened. I knew Sam better than anyone and should be able to find him. He was such a private and guarded man that many times I felt I didn't know him. But, God, how I loved him from the moment we first met. Another house-shaking clap of thunder jolts me back to the present.

I really should head to our basement bedroom if I'm to get any sleep tonight. I guess I could start reading through the three years of printed emails, bank statements, and files to search for clues.

James, Deputy Stark, says I'm clutching at straws now. I'm just desperately seeking an answer for where Sam is. If he is dead, I need to find him and give him a proper burial, for peace and closure. I can't believe he'll never return to me.

Lightning flashes through the basement window shade as I head down the stairs. My mind is playing tricks on me again- I swear I caught a glimpse of Sam in his favorite leather coat disappearing into the bedroom wall. I'm losing it. That coat, with his scent that I've cuddled in so many times, is in our upstairs bedroom closet. I must reassure myself it's still there and run up the stairs to check. It's missing! Is it possible he's alive and here? If so, why hasn't he come to me?

I'm rushing down the narrow basement stairs to check the wall when familiar arms grab me from behind and cover my mouth. Sam is alive! Relief and anger overwhelm me. Sam's hungry mouth covers my scream, and my only thought is I ache for his touch. His muscular arms easily lift my 5'2" petite frame and carry me to our iron bed. We come together in passionate lovemaking as if for the first time. The throes of ecstasy as our bodies come together erase the pain of the last two years. As we lie back, I'm brought back to reality.

"Where the hell have you been the last two years? Do you have a clue what I've been through?"

"'Shh, baby, I never wanted to hurt you, but I needed to get away from you."

"What the hell?"

"It was to protect you, baby... there are some truly evil people looking for me, and if they think you know anything, you're in terrible danger. I need you to declare me dead, claim the insurance money and move on without me. I'll know you're financially set and safe. You and our family will be safe. The less you know, the safer you are. That damned cursed Covid and travel restrictions screwed up my escape plans. This is the last time we'll talk. I didn't mean to reveal myself to you when I saw you; I lost all control."

We talked for hours before he disappeared in the civil war tunnels he'd discovered while working on our basement tornado sanctuary. With our final kiss, he had me vow to declare him dead, claim the insurance money, and open my heart to Deputy Sparks.

ART WILLIAM L. BREACH

◄◄ ◄◆► ►►

Native-born Texan, Art William L. Breach, grew up with the Franklin Mountains as his playground in the far west corner of the Lone Star State. There his love of the geosciences, specifically; paleontology was nurtured. He honed his academic and creative skills on rock outcroppings incessantly searching for fossils. Deeply inspired by the works of his mentor, H. P. Lovecraft, his imagination soared from the horror-infested gulfs of space to charnel depths where puffy worm things feast on the world's dead. Even in slumber the Dreamlands bade him explore and chart new territory. And so, he did and continues to do so.

But it doesn't end there. The spectrum of his influence includes a wide assortment of musical talent from

Tchaikovsky to Andy Williams and the genius of England's finest, The Moody Blues.

By day he works an administrative position with a well-established national company. On Wednesday evenings you can find him at church studying Scripture under pastoral leadership or having in-depth Bible studies while discipling and encouraging others. He is a devout scholar of all Scripture but favors Wisdom Literature *especially* Ecclesiastes.

Though currently residing in southwest Missouri, his heart firmly remains in El Paso, Texas.

JOURNAL FOUND IN THE
NORTHFIELD WOODS

*et out! Leave while you can! **RUN!** Don't you understand?!*

I hear them . . . their sick, horrible, wet-gurgling, sucking sounds in the woods.

-- Oh my God! They're here!

These six trees bear testimony to this final warning. Carved into the bark of each is a solitary letter denoting B-E-W-A-R-E.

I know the hideous truth! They were summoned from the dark spaces between the stars. Under the cover of night, they stalk on the winds. By day they burrow into subterraneous caverns where they are worshipped by things long dead.

In grotesque fascination, Alden Fisher closed the egregious journal abandoned to the Northfield Woods. Its unintentional discovery was instrumental in a quest for truth that never should have yielded tangible evidence. Oppressive, motionless air suffocated the region compounding its unnatural ambiance. Ice trickled through his veins. The carvings were eerie. . .ominous. Standing amidst the circle of trees screaming their deterrent message, he systematically gauged their merit while moving on a turnstile of madness, frantically begging, hoping, praying for something – *anything* to tell him that this was all. . . *unreal.*

With a sneakered foot, he prodded the mulch where the accursed volume had been entombed. Frantic handfuls of dead foliage and topsoil were clawed out. The journal was hastily pushed into the soft earth with leaves strewn to slightly conceal its intentional presence. Whoever did this clearly wanted it found. Moving tree to tree, he gingerly probed each carving, moving his fingers along the jagged edges. Desperation, not artistry, marked the hastily chiseled letters.

Dark thoughts, silently ravaging his mind, left him with one unwavering truth -- the love for his son. Timmy's frantic account of what he saw in the Northfield Woods was disquieting as a stroll through an exhumed graveyard. Inexorably his grandfather's pocket watch ticked away in roaring silence, the minutes that turned to hours.

Knock-knock. . .knock-knock, muscled its way through Alden's crowded mind. Acceptance sought entrance at logic's door. A detested thing demanding an audience. *No! This isn't real – it can't be.* Though brushed aside, residuals remained on the doorstep.

The crackling of the underbrush marked Alden's footfalls as he ventured through the otherwise muted woods. A strange brook came into view, narrowing as it meandered into the distance. Fond childhood memories of southern New Mexico's woodlands entered with soothing refrains of babbling brooks incorporated into nature's orchestrated outdoors. A nervous smile came but departed. This brooklet neither coursed nor babbled, nor revealed whence it flowed, nor did it bear highland tales; nothing remained to proclaim the life taken from it.

"Daddy! I don't like it here! I'm scared! There's something in the woods that's very bad! I wanna go home!" Timmy had been inconsolable despite Alden's firm, comforting embrace. Initially puzzled – *he's only an eight-year-old boy prone to imagination* – Alden held Timmy tightly, fighting against the growing root of dread entwining systemically through him. *He saw a bear or a deer. Something familiar startled him. His fertile imagination transformed it into an unspeakable horror. THAT'S IT!. . .It has to be.* Timmy was a good kid, well-raised. He *never* lied. That fact incrementally gnawed his sanity to shreds.

Timmy's unhinging from reality had been days ago. Its intensity escalated. Days of sheer panic bled into nights of psychosis. Shrieks in the wee hours of the morning from down the hall sent him and his wife bolting towards Timmy's bedroom where, in wide-eyed terror, he had taken refuge under his desk. The sparkle of innocence was shattered. Joyful laughter was replaced with muffled whimpering. At day's end, there was no solace. Now only a father's quest remained.

He vowed before God and his son that he'd scout the woods. The question lingered: how to convince an unreasonable child that monsters aren't real. The lack of tangible proof of his son's claim would be *the* conclusive evidence. Nothing amiss was going to be revealed. But that was presumptuous. The claim itself demanded corroborating evidence in either direction.

Fear decisively moved its ravenous army in a death march toward a concerned father's tender heart. A nervous sweat beaded his brow. He was being watched. Malevolent eyes forged in dark, infinite knowledge and timeless as the gulfs of space tore through his soul leaving him as palpably defiled as the surrounding earth. A presence of chaotic evil marred him. *Nerves*, he thought, though this ran deeper.

Mere emotion didn't defile a man.

Alden hastened his pace along the brooklet's winding course where neither fern nor flower flourished. Morning lapsed into early afternoon. Eager eyes swept expectantly for signs of normalcy. Nothing in nature's repertoire offered consolation. Nothing that flew, crept, or crawled, slithered or burrowed, scampered, or otherwise walked through the blighted landscape manifested itself.

Hope edged him onward through the backswing of a celestial scythe that grimly reaped everything in its path. A once luxuriant environment defiantly died before him. Macabre thoughts dangled from his mind's rafters. He snatched one. A back-page article in an Ozarks newspaper, some days prior to Timmy's return from camp, related that several mangled bodies had been found. The carnage was attributed to bears. Names withheld pending notification of next of kin. Official reports were classified. Though tragic, he was grateful that some fifty miles in distance separated the two events.

Unnaturally silent, yet in majestic splendor, the sloping Ozarks rose and fell fantastically to nature's rhythms. The panoramic view swelled in contradictory terms of life and death, survival and defeat, innocence and defilement.

Previously undetected, due to natural angles in the terrain, an orifice into the Earth left him rapt with its incongruity. Collegiately trained in the geosciences, the hollow bore no markings of any natural formation. Angst knotted his stomach. Reluctance inched him forward. The day drew weary. Shadows lengthened. It was getting late. In early autumn day, yielded to night's demands in the hill country. Furtively he scanned the terrain leading to Earth's gaping wound. Another hellish denizen from the rafters pointed a gnarled finger toward him.

The journal!

Reaching behind him, he pulled out the offensive manuscript. Its random gibberish, blurted in jumbled, distorted thoughts with hastily drawn images, lunged from the pages. Quickly thumbing its nefarious contents, he searched . . .

Great burrows secretly are digged into the charnel clay where porous terrain should suffice. Things below have learned to walk that ought to creep. Don't approach them. The nethermost caverns are not for the fathoming of eyes to see. Their marvels are damnable! Strange and terrific.

Fear the night. That's when they move. Feel their presence here, even by day. Death rides the winds with them.

Horrible! Horrible! They're dead! ALL dead! NOT human! – they NEVER were. . . My God! I can't bear to look upon them. Madness resides here. It clings to the forest like a diseased growth. The Earth vomits their essence into the air.

Listen to me! When the shadows deepen to nightfall, they stir. MOVE! --

Through the preponderance of unexpected evidence, a macabre puzzle with its interlocking pieces came together. Timmy's wild rantings, the word B-E-W-A-R-E maniacally carved into the trees, a bedeviled glen, that damned journal, and the yawning chasm whispering his name. Snapping it closed, the thing was returned to the back pocket of his jeans.

The nameless dread reposing in that yawning void had to be confronted. Here all matters culminated. Darkness was imminent. It was now or never. Commitment demanded an answer. Tree limbs eerily contorted to grasping bony claws like ghoulish appendages pushing out of fetid graves.

*Get out! Leave while you can! **RUN!** Don't you understand?!*

Scanning the horizon, he calculated how long it would take him to return to where he had parked. Dusk would have settled before he could make it to the SUV, providing he left then. If he explored that place, with its accompanying secrets, no telling. Resolutely he moved deeper into the Ozarks' embrace, pausing for a moment.

"Timmy, Adriel. . . I love you. Honey, take good care of our son."

He proceeded to the gaping entrance observing that this hadn't been chiseled by machinery, nor had it been caused by natural erosion. This was the result of bioturbation at an incalculable level. *What did this?*

A miasma of belching gas emanating from the bowels of the earth accosted Alden. Turning his head, he backed away from the entrance until the nausea abated. Inching his way into the yawning chasm, a low monotone whistling made its way from Erebus depths. *Wind, no doubt.* A pocket flashlight, navigating unfamiliar terrain, sent darkness scampering a hasty retreat from the only revelatory light that reprehensible place had ever known.

As he progressed, an unwelcoming pulsating glitter incrementally filled the tunnel's throat. Erudition bowed its head to unfamiliarity. *A light. Origin unknown.* A glow of – *color?. . .* Its consuming textures and wavelengths shone outside the spectrum of descriptive reasoning.

Movement up ahead. Hideous contorted shadows forged by corporeal abominations stretched on the path toward him. Startled, he flicked his thumb dousing the light while stumbling back into one of the numerous cavern crevices praying fervently to avoid detection. Holding his breath in the dark, he waited expectantly. Things of nightmares shambled past. His eyes stung bitterly at the putrescence emanating from the loathsome horde. Grateful for the presence of consuming shadow, he bided his time.

Dear God! Please let me get out of here alive! My family!

In the darkness, acceptance of the impossible strengthened him. Dissonant bellowing moans emanating from the entrance rousted him from that secretive hiding place. Abandoning reason's sense to flee, he descended the stygian depths where pulsating globules of odious slime lined the path indicating points of contact. Knowledge prodded him as a child would a poisonous arachnid. The writhing, flopping, ghoulish forms had taken to the wing. Sticky-wet, flapping sloshes grotesquely indicated their departure.

A low-frequency vibration rumbled beneath him. At first, *tremor* came to mind only to be dismissed. The study of seismic activity he knew well. This had an altogether different feel. Scattered twigs of sanity strewn across the wastelands of his mind snapped where hypothesis trampled through. The turning beneath escalated. Alden nearly toppled onto the slime-smeared passageway. A reflexive hand shot out, grabbing a rock outcropping.

The nefarious manifestation vomited into his memory thoughts of New England. Begrudged time at Arkham's Miskatonic University. Research on questionable paleontological findings from their disastrous 1930 Antarctic expedition. Impossible contradictory geological notes and samples. Obscure forbidden volumes denied access to all, barring the elect. The abhorred *Journal of Aben Schavel. . . De Vermis Mysteriis. . . the Necronomicon*; others corroborating the incomprehensible. A juxtapositional study concluding delusion against fact. A wasted semester soon forgotten. . . until its resurgence.

The mysteries of the worm. Those ponderous archaic volumes spanning ages whispered insanely from moldy parchment of detestable subservient winged hybrids. World devourers turning, grinding, destroying from within.

The small flashlight became unnecessary in the unnatural hues of phosphorescence. It was pocketed by a white-knuckled hand. Sound perceived initially as wind became increasingly distinct as a woodwind lacking in pitch. Rounding a bend through serpentine corridors, the passageway opened to a mammoth chamber. He shivered against the things revealed there, for he did not like them. Necrotic titan toadstools, jutting offensively from corrupt soil, writhed to the maddening monotone pipping. Across the infernal court's vast expanse, in a cleft concealed mostly from dull illumination, an ill-cowled atrocity flopped obscenely playing a makeshift flute. Its form alluded to an octopoid batrachian obscenity mingled with chiropteran features. Tentacles on its back caused the concealing garment to undulate in a ghastly manner.

And beneath those abhorrent sights and others, in sunken chambers, tunneled worm-things of immense proportion. Unnatural subterranean dwellers bearing little to no resemblance to antiquity's *Lumbricus terrestris*.

The madness of his screams drove him from Tartarean depths before the pest-gulfs could bring to bear all their charnel legions upon him.

◆

He neither recalled when or how he returned home. The details of his hospitalization were later recounted to him. While institutionalized in the trying hours of isolation, a passage from the *Journal of Aben Schavel,* scribed in Middle Latin, surfaced. He transcribed it from memory as best possible.

"Deceitful are the practices of day. Fear the time. For corrupt life concealed swells from the charnel earth to vex manifest creation. Loathsome are the star walkers who fell from of old. What we perceive by sense in reality is illusion. I declare that the dead are more fortunate than the living. Better than all are the still who have not been, for they will never know the evil committed under the sun."

THE SINISTER HOUSE AT
WYRN'S DEPOT

Sinister shapes undulated in the forged eerie, low-lying mist blanketing the landscape to whims of stale night air. In nightmarish cadence, they performed ancient dance rituals around rotted, gnarled trees jutting out of the earth that had long ago rejected them. A high gibbous moon in sickly, pale light washed the leprous terrain in ghastly illumination.

On a long and winding road, in the forgotten recesses of that hill country, a slow-moving vehicle made its reluctant way into the unknown. Twin beams of light peered into the night's gloom creating elongated shadows.

Dan Warner's flesh crawled. He scanned the inhospitable surroundings. Cautiously he maneuvered his '65 hardtop across the dark, uninviting country. Each cough and sputter gave reproach that maintenance should've been addressed prior to meeting with the firm's reclusive client.

Who the hell in their right mind would live out here?

Matters didn't always go like clockwork in his world. Upward mobility, despite intentional efforts, was one of them. With diligence, he handled his casework. There had to be another firm that would take him. He had paid his dues. It was time to move on. The contract binding him to the practice neared renewal. Not a chance. Both senior partners in the firm were going to get an earful when he returned.

Dumb shit! No! I'll do it later! He berated himself while the jalopy bounced along on unpaved backroads. But later never came. He procrastinated one too many times.

He cursed under his breath as "Old Faithful" coughed, sputtered and died on a gravel road on the outskirts of Wyrn's Depot. That was the last time it would ever run. It had gone its final mile.

A swirling vortex of madness lurked at the threshold. Biding its time in the prison's darkness, it waited and watched.

Something approached. It was human.

Brooding in the broken-down heap on the roadside, his mind played out multiple scenarios searching for the most viable option. He tried starting it up again. Nothing. Necessity demanded action though intuition bade him stay.

Stupid! Of course!

He eagerly grabbed his phone off the dashboard. No signal. He tossed the dead phone onto the passenger seat with a sigh.

Shit! No fucking car and no phone! What next?

He slammed his fists on the steering wheel.

Think! When was the last time you passed a gas station or a mom-and-pop store? What a place for the freakin' car to break down in! Shit!

THWUMP!

A blow to the passenger side broke his focused

concentration. The jarring motion shattered his pretense of calm.

What the hell!?

Locked doors offered brief, hesitant security. Peering over the driver's side and not seeing anything, he stretched over as far as possible to the passenger side under the seat belt's restraint.

He sat alone in an unnatural sea of frothing mist. His calculating law-school-trained mind left him bewildered.

I nodded off then jarred awake.

A thin tendril of hope seized the fleeing thought before it escaped.

I can't stay here indefinitely.

He unbuckled the safety belt.

Don't go out there.

I have to.

He reached over his shoulder and unlocked the door.

Fear is largely an illusion of the mind.

Stretching as far as the eye could see, there was only the grayness of decay. Fear shadowed him. He didn't want to leave the car's security, but time was a pressing factor. He got down and closed the unlocked door behind him.

Don't forget the flashlight.

Stopping, abruptly turning, he opened the door and knelt on the seat reaching across to the glove compartment and he removed his flashlight. The door closed behind him with a click. Before resolutely advancing, it was tested.

Stay here till the break of day.

I'm on deadline. There's nothing to be afraid of.

If the guys at the firm could only see him now.

Assholes!

Over a power lunch some months ago, the topic of local folklore arose. It passed the time and served to amuse. Large New England city temperaments sneered at backwater superstition.

He froze dead in his tracks. Distraction fled. He whipped

around and then back again, attempting to take in all that his flashlight revealed.

Where am I?!

The night's eerie silence greeted him. Having traversed some distance, his meandering thoughts kept his feet moving through the malefic surrealism of the God-forsaken night.

Anemic moonlight filtered through the heavy night air. All around, the mist continued its grotesque, macabre undulations around long-dead trees like indecorous children playing between gravestones.

A light in the distance. *A will-o'-the-wisp? No.* Between the gnarled branches, a light flickered. His shallow breathing permeated the tomblike silence.

A clearing came into view. Rotted branches tugged at his clothing. Relentlessly he pressed on against their hindrance on him to venture no further. A sweaty palm gripped the flashlight, searching for bearings with each illuminated swipe.

He broke through the clearing casting a furtive glance over his shoulder, grateful to be free from the woods' influence. An erratic sigh escaped from between dry, parted lips. Some three hundred feet in the distance, a cold, unwelcoming frame caused him to recoil.

It squatted in forlorn disrepair, ancient and decrepit as a testimony to time's inexorable march. Protruding from the earth as a corpse's anatomy might from an ill-made grave, the structure jutted, complimenting the rotted hill country. Laid waste by the ravages of time and neglect, it waited.

He fought against the mounting anxiety gnawing at him to run.

Closer said the spider to the fly. . .

Quick! While there's still a chance – run! For the love of God – run! No matter what, don't look back!

No! Press on. Yield no ground.

Adrenaline coursed through him as he gained yardage

incrementally.

He couldn't shake the feeling with certainty that *something* was seriously wrong. He was somehow being *led* there.

Closer. . .

In dull despair, cold, uninviting, grimy windows stared out into the night. With **his** proximity to the structure came the sound of unhinged dangling weathered shutters banging against rotted wood planks.

Again, he paused. He was being watched. He knew it. He squirmed, ill at ease with the feeling that *something* in that house was watching his every move.

Closer. . .

The night held its breath. He stared at the crumbling wreck that whispered his name. He advanced as a moth inexorably drawn to the flame.

Termite infestation had long ago done its share of the ravaging. Curled flecks of paint littered the porch. Fragments of molding strewn on the ground protruded out of the low-lying mist. He kicked them aside to clear a path to the short, crumbling staircase. He waved the flashlight's beam frantically, attempting to shed light on hidden clues reposing in the deep shadows. Anemic moonlight offered no assistance in the quest for illumination.

In the past, the old house might have been inviting, warm, and friendly. The front porch swing, half resting on an uneasy edge on the splintered porch, dangled by a single, rusted chain from the sagging roof. He ruminated over a possible spring day long ago when a happy couple might have sat in that very swing holding hands while contemplating their years together.

He tested the front steps, uncertain if they would bear his weight. They creaked their resentment as he committed to them. Sweeping the flashlight's beam across its dilapidated surface, he approached the oval windowed front door. No light emanated from within. But there *had* been a light. He took a handkerchief from his pocket and wiped at the ornately chiseled smoke-colored glass panel. Dusty grime came off, leaving deep streaks preventing him from peering into the mysterious abode.

He rehearsed what he would say in the event that someone should answer, though he knew no one would.

He knocked on the front door. Each thud echoed eerily. He tried the doorknob. It yielded to his efforts. An ominous scream from rusted hinges informed the darkness that there was a new presence entering its domain.

The front parlor alone was an antiquarian's dream. The place hadn't been touched. Layers of dust and grime attested that the dwelling had not been disturbed in a very long time. Whatever happened here had caused the inhabitants to flee and not return for their personal belongings.

As he entered the front room, motes of dust swirled upward, causing him to sneeze. He called out, hoping to be greeted. Only silence replied.

Portraits hanging in ornate frames stared from the past, compounding to his discomfort. He trained the flashlight beam on each one, in turn scanning the walls and surrounding areas. They were repulsive. Something they had seen or knew only too well had been captured for all time.

Closer. . .

A staircase to his left, almost across from the front door, caught his attention. More portraits adorned the wall beside the staircase and each bearing the same strain of madness. Young and old alike.

He mounted the stairs, wondering what secrets were held captive in each room after jealously being guarded for so long. Darkness gave way to the light after displacing its undisturbed dominion after so long. Gaining the top landing, the sound of the front door closing reached him, causing him to nearly drop the flashlight in response.

Pausing with bated breath, he listened intently. No sound of movement emanated from below.

Where did that light come from?

Rooms lined either side of the long upstairs hallway. At the far end, pale moonlight, which was neither comforting nor beautiful, filtered through a grimy window. Specters glided effortlessly through the long corridor. Shadows, no doubt, from the gnarled willow outside. He passed the light from side to side down the hallway listening for movement. He would have to search room by room. The thought lacked appeal.

Drawn to the last room to the left, would be as good a place as any to start. Frayed carpeting muffled his passage. He moved fearfully past each closed door.

He paused with his hand on the doorknob. The last room upstairs.

Through the dust covering, memories of long ago whispered into the barren night. Each item held its own piece of nostalgia. He took them in one by one. A mirror hanging on the far wall opposite the chamber door caught his attention. He had never seen anything quite like it before. The peculiar thing that it was, it held no reflective properties. Its surface was more like a highly polished obsidian. The highly ornate gold frame alone would fetch an attractive price.

He inched his way toward it. The light oddly enough didn't reflect on its surface. The thing became more loathsome. It was an obscenity. Despite its potential market value, he recoiled from it. Horrid, indescribable things of an indeterminable origin adorned the frame. Ill-formed orbs stared at him. They were aware of the intruder's presence.

From the center of the mirror, a gaseous funnel formed. Things depicted on the bas-relief etchings on the frame moved in the mirror's violent, raging depths. Staring in disbelief, he stood transfixed, staring uncomprehendingly at the surface of the mirror displaying a hellish nightmare within. His mouth opened into a silent scream that never left his throat. It had been cut short by appendages emanating from within the mirror's uncharted gulfs. Monstrosities without true form constricted him with crushing force. The flashlight was sent spinning off striking a large chest some feet away.

In the final moments of his life, he failed to find acceptance in the reality of the inconceivable.

Something vaguely resembling what once had been Dan Warner twitched with life and picked itself up off the floor. The obsidian-like mirror that hung in the last room in an old, abandoned house in the deep, dark woods was carried away. Turning, it moved toward the door, down the hallway and descended the stairs holding one set of footprints – the final testament of Dan Warner's life.

The front door opened once more. Stepping out and down the stairs, the thing gazed into the obsidian surface. It stood briefly glaring balefully at the moon as it remembered stars and worlds beyond telescopic reach before it took wing, returning to the timeless gulfs from whence it came. Others awaited. The gate had been rendered.

JAMES R. WILDER

◄◄ ◄◆► ►►

James R. Wilder, a retired journalist, uses his experiences as a police-beat newspaper reporter and an automotive editor when writing his short story "who-dun-its." In addition, he is known for his contemporary western Harbison Mystery Series novels. He resides in Springfield, Missouri.

www.harbisonmysteryseries.com
http://www.swggoodreads.org

COLORS OF CONFUSION

The roar of a four-barrel carburetor kicking in on an Oldsmobile 324 cubic-inch Rocket engine isn't much of a surprise if you like performance cars. Having it pointed at me as the driver tromped the gas pedal brought out a whole different emotion—I was scared shitless.

How the hell did I get into this mess?

I came back to Elmhurst last week after my mother passed away unexpectedly. Mom made it to age 86 without any major problems—and then she was gone, dying in her sleep. I wish I could go that way. She drew a crowd at the funeral home visitation and even more of her friends showed up for the funeral mass at St. Mary's. I hadn't seen many of them in years. Father O'Connell said some nice words, even if his homily was a little too long.

Sally called me at Mom's house the next day while I was packing some of her things. She apologized for her absence at the services and abruptly changed the subject asking for a small favor. Surely, I could do that for an old flame—even if she dumped me a month or so after I joined the Marines. Most of us signed up for the service following the attack on Pearl Harbor. She took no time in marrying one of the few men granted a deferment because he was needed to keep his parents' scrap-metal business running. At least, that's what our congressman's letter to the draft board said.

I was impressed when I pulled up to the address she'd given me in the ritzy part of town. The three-story brick and limestone mansion was built by a riverboat captain more than 50 years earlier to resemble the vessel that had made him a fortune on the Mississippi. It had a manicured lawn of Zosia grass, trimmed hedges, and marigolds in bloom. Once inside, everything looked brand new but with Victorian charm.

Sally dressed like many women of the country club set, wearing a light-cotton flowered summer dress with a halter top, along with a pair of decorative wedged sandals on her feet. She greeted me with a kiss on the cheek. She was reserved compared to the going away present she gave me in the back seat of my old Plymouth back in January of '42.

"We need your help, Red. My daughter, Julie is missing."

While she spoke, I stared at the family portrait hanging over the huge fireplace. It was nearly 6 feet wide and 4 feet high. The teenager in the photo presented more of a smirk than a smile and I had a hard time trying to figure out what parent she favored.

"We?" I asked.

"My husband, Earl and I. You remember him? Earl Langston. He was on the football team with you."

Yeah, I remembered him from back then. He only made the team because his old man was a sports booster who bought uniforms and equipment for us. And for some reason, the coach got a new car our senior year. Langston held down the bench most of the time and was only put in to play when we were beating our opponents by enormous leads.

"Why me? Call the cops. I've been selling paint to body shops since the war ended."

"But you were in the military police in the service. Surely you have the expertise to help get her back."

"The work I normally did back then involved finding passed-out drunks who hadn't come back from their furloughs."

Earl interrupted. He'd been sitting in the living room reading the newspaper while smoking a long Cuban cigar. He managed to lift himself out of his chair and walk over to join his wife.

"We prefer not to call the police. Julie's been in trouble before and we don't need our names plastered in the papers again. She's a brat. She's lit out in her car before, but we found a note on our doorstep this time."

He handed me a piece of loose-leaf paper that had cut-out letters in different sizes and colors from magazines pasted to it. It reminded me of an episode of Richard Diamond Private Detective, but I don't think anyone with a mug like mine would mistake me for actor David Janssen.

"I need $10,000 if you want to see your daughter again. Have one of your low-level workers walk to the corner of Water Street and Maine at midnight for the trade."

"Low-level worker?"

"That's the majority of my employees," Earl said. "You'll pass for one." Then he handed me a zippered bank bag filled with cash.

"Don't try to run off with this, or I'll send some 'real' detectives after you."

Like Sally, Earl Langston was only about 33 or 34 years old, but the bald spot on the crown of his head stood out from his dark-brown hair. If he had bangs, he would have looked like Robin Hood's Friar Tuck. His physique wasn't lacking either if he was ever asked to portray Richard Greene's sidekick in the TV series. Either Sally became a great cook, or the two ate out a lot. Sally on the other hand didn't look much different than she did when she was in high school. The big change was that her strawberry-blonde hair was bleached to platinum. When I mentioned it, she explained that it was "all the rage," especially since many thought it made her look like Marilyn Monroe.

"What kind of car does she drive?"

"It's a two-tone '55 Olds two-door hardtop, charcoal and pink," Earl said.

"General Motors calls it Juneau gray and coral," I noted.

He wasn't impressed with my knowledge of automotive paint.

◆━◆━◆

The night was hot and muggy. Fog filled the air after an evening's summer rain and steam rose up from the ancient pavement. It looked like more rain was on the way. My bullet-nosed Studebaker's wool upholstery was more pungent than usual. I parked it halfway up Main Avenue and hiked the rest of the way to Water Street. As I walked, I could hear the waves of the Big Muddy rushing up against the flood walls to my left. Water Street was more like an alley. It was one of the few cobblestone streets left in town and was without streetlights. The sidewalk, only on one side of the road, was narrow and uneven. You could break your leg if you didn't watch where you were going.

It started to drizzle again about the same time that I reached my destination. I pulled up the collar of my Robert Hall all-weather coat and pulled down the brim of my fedora to keep the rain off of my neck and face. I laughed at myself. Maybe I was more like Phillip Marlowe than Richard Diamond.

Then I heard the roar of the car and saw it heading right for me. I stood frozen in the street as the Olds Super 88 screeched to a halt with the rear wheels locking up as it skidded to a stop only inches in front of me. The driver, slight in size, reached out a hand for the money. I grabbed their arm with my left hand and shoved the barrel of my

Model 1911 Colt up against the driver's skull.

It was Julie.

"Who the hell are you?" she snarled.

"Your ride home. Scoot over, honey."

Julie was embarrassed as we approached the front steps of her stately manner as the rain started to pour down in buckets. I had my hand wrapped around her wrist so she wouldn't try to make a run for it. Her mother, with tears in her eyes, hugged her.

"I thought you were gone forever," she said.

Earl took his time walking up behind his wife. He shrugged his shoulders, first looking at me, and then at Julie. "That red hair of yours is a mess," he said as he headed in the direction of the living room where I could hear the buzz of the TV that was shared with the after hour's test pattern on the screen. Julie showed an expression of distaste for her father's comments and then told her mother she was going upstairs to her room.

I handed the unopened bank bag to Sally. She looked up at me and smiled.

"She's quite a handful," I noted.

"Yes she is. I also think her hair is beautiful. Don't you? It's just like yours," she said.

THE GRIT

T he young woman, while attractive, looked more like a pixie as she strolled along the side of the pool shared by guests of the LINQ and Harrah's hotels in Las Vegas. She was looking for an empty lounge chair.

Seth Eakin gazed over at the woman, unbeknownst to her. His mirrored aviator sunglasses prevented her from seeing his interest in her. She stood not more than 5 feet tall, and her auburn hair was cut short, much like that of actress Keira Knightley. As she got closer, he began to notice the simplicity of her beauty—much different from many of the women already at the pool. She wore single diamond-chip earrings without any other noticeable piercings and what showed of her skin was absent of tattoos. Her fingernails were manicured and only covered with clear polish. She stood out mainly because of her bright red lipstick. Although attractive, her chest was as flat as a pancake. He still found her to be beautiful.

As she approached, it looked as if she was pointing at Eakin. Then he realized that the young woman was asking if the lounge chair next to him was taken. He put down his book.

"Help yourself."

"Thank you so much. I was afraid I'd have to lay out my towel on the concrete."

Eakin smiled as he went back to his book. The woman rifled through her beach bag retrieving a tube of Coppertone sunscreen and her iPhone. She laid down on her stomach and undid the back of her top. Her bikini was modest to say the least, with high-rise-waist bottoms. The top, which was laying underneath her chest, had more than enough material to cover her breasts.

Eakin was back with his nose in his book. It took his mind off of some near-future plans that were frustrating to him.

"Excuse me, I hate to bother you, but could you put some sunscreen on my back."

Expecting him to accept, she had the tube of SPF 30 already reached out in his direction.

Eakin looked at the SPF rating, reached into his own bag and retrieved an aerosol can of the same SPF and brand, spraying it over her back."

"You didn't have to use yours," she said, somewhat startled by the act. "I have another tube in my bag."

"It's not that," Eakin said. "I didn't want to look like a lecherous old man pawing over a young woman. Besides, I didn't want to get any of the lotion on the book I'm reading."

"Well, thank you. I'm Susan Ward. I just finished with the Consumer Electronics Show at the Las Vegas Convention Center. I decided to take a couple of more days off. I'm on my own dime now so I elected to stay at the LINQ, instead of the Venetian. I didn't know the pool area here was so small."

"I'm Seth Eakin. I just finished up with a fiction-writers convention at the Bellagio. Like you, I'm at the LINQ because I'm on my own dime."

"Oh, and by the way," she chuckled. "I don't think you look like a lecherous old man. I think you look very handsome."

"Well, I'm fifty-eight years old and I imagine you're not much over twenty-two or twenty-three."

Susan said she was nearly 27 and held the position of a computer programmer for a company in Kansas City. Eakin listened intently as she continued to talk. She had broken up with her boyfriend of three months, and the extra weekend in Vegas was planned to give her a breather. She liked how Eakin seemed to listen so intently instead of bragging about his own job. She also noticed that his left hand was absent from a wedding band or the indentation that showed one had been removed recently.

Then she began to question him. He tried to be humble so she wouldn't think he was wealthy.

"I've been a newspaper copywriter for most of my life, writing mystery novels on the side. After ten years I finally made it to the big leagues with a bestseller. The group asked me to be a guest speaker and encourage those who were not yet successful to continue their efforts."

Susan was intrigued, he thought as she continued to ask more questions. She learned that his book was titled *The Murder Inferno*. He reached into his own beach bag for a copy.

"Here, it's autographed" he said as he handed it to her.

She thumbed through the book and then read the description on the inside flap and Eakin's short biography on the back cover.

"You don't have your photo in the back section."

"Well, I independently published this. I didn't think my photo was important. It's not likely that my mug shot would increase book sales. The cover illustration was more important to the plot. I paid quite a bit to the artist who designed it."

Susan felt very comfortable talking with him. She figured someone like him would be an easy catch for a younger woman like herself. Then she got up her nerve to make sure she could keep his attention.

"Do you think there are any rules about sunning topless here?"

Eakin tried to stay composed.

"I don't know what the rules are. But 'what goes on in Vegas, stays in Vegas,'" he responded quietly.

She turned over and slathered some lotion on her chest.

"Well, I'm in the back corner of the pool area away from nearly everyone except you. If I wipe off my lipstick and keep my sunglasses on, maybe everyone will think I'm a young man wearing a pair of Speedos. Nobody ever accused me of being a full-figure girl."

Eakin tried not to stare even though his sunglasses would hide his eyes. He admired what he considered her bravery. She was confident in herself and her actions. To be honest, it was the type of woman he had an interest in.

Within 15 minutes, a female lifeguard in a one-piece red bathing suit marched over to the back corner of the pool area.

"Ma'am, I'm sorry, but topless sunbathing is not allowed here. You'll have to cover up."

Eakin felt his new friend should be defended.

"Miss, I'm a close friend of Henry Marks, the director of this establishment, and he assured me there would be no problem when my friend took full advantage of this sunny day as long as she stayed away from the mainstream of guests. I'll gladly accompany you to his office to settle this manner."

The lifeguard was stunned. She paused.

"I'm sorry to have disturbed you."

Then she ambled away.

"I saw the man's photo and title by the registration desk. I didn't know if the lifeguard would fall for my story or not."

Susan thought his move was hilarious. Then she continued to question her new friend. She sat up so they could see each other eye-to-eye. It showed she trusted him. Eakin felt more comfortable telling his life history to her and he didn't mind the view. He had divorced more than 10 years ago. His wife constantly voiced her disapproval of his weekly paycheck and his writing, which took up all of his spare time. She finally filed for divorce and had gone through two other husbands since.

"She took me for practically everything I had—even my dog."

His ex-wife made contact with him for the first time since the divorce when Eakin's book hit the best-seller list, saying she thought they should get together again. He politely declined.

Two hours went by quickly for Susan and for Eakin as well. He ordered a couple of beers for them. He paid in cash, opting not to add it to his hotel bill. She noticed a number of one-hundred dollar bills in his wallet as he fished out a twenty for the beer.

"I hope you won't find me too forward," she said. "Will you join me tonight? I've wanted to go to Toby Keith's and try its special meatloaf, and I've got two tickets for Santana. I bought them before my break-up."

Eakin hesitated, explaining that he was really fond of her but that many women had suddenly become attracted to him after his book's success. The interests in him were artificial, with money being their main motive for a relationship. And of course, there was the age difference.

"Just think of it as two friends out on the town going Dutch treat," she said. "You can pay for dinner and drinks, and I've already paid for the concert tickets."

Eakin scratched his chin.

"Okay, but I'll pay for the taxi to and from Mandalay Bay and the cost of dinner. I'll meet you at six down in the hotel lobby."

She picked up her bikini top and put it in her beach bag and positioned the towel around her neck, draping it over her chest, as she waved goodbye. To Eakin, the view of her walking away was just as appealing as when she'd approached him.

◆ ◢◤ ◆

Eakin, wearing a blue blazer, grey slacks, and an open-collar shirt, waved to Susan as she approached. She wore what many women referred to as a little black dress. But instead of high heels she wore flats. She didn't want to be thrown off balance as she walked.

The evening was everything the couple had hoped for. It felt like they had known each other for years. As the cab pulled into the underground entrance to the LINQ, Susan leaned over and whispered into Eakin's ear.

"Will you stay with me tonight?"

The expression on Eakin's face showed that of surprise and gratification. Again, he paused.

"Why not my room?"

Perhaps Eakin's mistrust of money-hungry women had contributed to his small request. Susan had heard stories of men waking up with their companions gone, as well as their cash and credit cards. Maybe he planned to put his wallet in the small safe inside the hotel-room closet. Hopefully he didn't think that of her even though they had only known each other for less than a day.

"Here's my key card," Eakin said. "I have a bottle of rosé on the counter. Make yourself comfortable. I have to make one call and I'll be right up. I'll knock four times, pause, and knock four more times so you'll know it's really me."

Susan embraced him and kissed him on the lips for the first time.

"Don't be long. I'll be waiting."

She rushed out of the cab and scurried to the elevator. Eakin stood on the sidewalk and made his call, still smiling as he talked.

◆

Three hours later, the man known to Susan as Seth Eakin, stood at the hotel concierge's desk at Harrah's Resort.

"I hope your stay here has been enjoyable, Mr. Sylvester. The bell boy will take your luggage to the limo when it arrives in about five minutes. And here's the envelope that was left for you a short time ago."

Eakin placed the thick envelope inside his jacket without opening it.

And they thought I couldn't pull it off. I didn't even have to invite her to spend the night, she invited me. The conquest is great, but the chase is even more exhilarating—especially at my age.

Hours later, Susan began to wake up. She was drowsy and her ears felt pressure until they popped. Zip ties confined her wrists to the armrests inside a Lear jet. As she looked out the window she saw the plane descend onto an airstrip in a desert landscape. Two men wearing traditional Arab headwear and robes sat across from her. One was holding an iPhone.

"I sent your photo to our Sheikh. He agrees you are a fine specimen—perfect for introducing his son to manhood."

MARGARITE STEVER

Margarite Stever grew up in Asbury, a tiny Missouri town of just over 200 people. She has a Bachelor of Arts Degree in English from Missouri Southern State University. She writes stories and essays that touch a person's heart. She is a member of Joplin Writers' Guild, Missouri Writers Guild, Sleuths' Ink Mystery Writers, serves on the board of Ozarks Writers League, and is Vice President of Ozarks Romance Authors. She published her short story collection, *Moonbeams and Ashes*, in October 2021. Her work has recently appeared in *Romance, Poetry, Mystery and More: An Anthology by Ozarks Romance Authors Members, Chicken Soup for the Soul: It's Beginning to Look a Lot Like Christmas;* Joplin Writers' Guild Anthology, *Seasons of the Four States; Anthology 2019 Sleuths' Ink Mystery*

Writers; *Missouri's Emerging Writers*; *Legends: Passion Pages*; *50-Word Stories* website; the 2021, 2019, 2018, 2017, and 2016 issues of *The Crowder Quill;* the Fall 2015 issue of *The Maine Review; Mamalode Magazine's 2015 Better Together;* and *Writer's Digest 2014 Show Us Your Shorts Collection.*

You can visit her website at www.margaritestever.com. Her seeds of wisdom and joy can be seen on her blog at http://ozarksmaven.com/, which has been read in over 90 countries.

LARRY THE LECHEROUS

"**O**ur Christmas party will be at McGuire's Irish Pub. I expect to see you there." My lecherous boss patted my rear. "Sweet Molly McGuire Wine Cellar has a fabulous selection."

"I don't want to go, Larry," I said.

"You will go or you're fired. Then you'd lose your health insurance." He laughed. "Your dismissal wouldn't bother me at all. Broads like you are a dime a dozen." He slowly ran his hand over my butt. "Wear something sexy."

I silently cursed my leukemia, expensive medicine, and my horrible boss.

"Does your wife know you do this? That you cheat on her with unwilling employees?" I could not let this man get the better of me. I needed a job not this kind of abuse.

"She knows her place. She is my wife. I'm head of the household. She doesn't get to dictate to me." He straightened his tie. "Bottom line is if you want to keep your job, you have to be a team player. I'm the team captain, so I call all the shots. Be at the bar by 7:00 p.m. or else."

I prepared carefully, laying out my supplies before slipping into my black cocktail dress. I arrived early and waited at the bar.

Larry walked in with his best buddy, Mike, the Human Resources Director. The two of them propositioned both the hostess and their waitress. The smart women turned them down.

I wondered how those two looked at themselves in the mirror. Hoping they wouldn't see me, I turned my back on them. It didn't work.

"Tina, get that luscious booty over here and join us," Larry said.

I took a deep breath to calm my nerves. I knew without a doubt what had to be done. I slipped into the chair on Larry's left, opposite the bar.

"What are you drinking?" Mike asked.

I held my glass of wine aloft. "Riesling."

Larry snorted. "Can't handle anything stronger, huh?"

Bristling, I chose my words carefully. "McGuire's Irish Pub is world-renowned for its wine. I would never dream of drinking anything else while I'm here. It would be a waste of opportunity."

Larry leaned close and whispered, "We'll have plenty of opportunity later."

He had no idea. Instead of voicing that thought, I shrugged my shoulder. "The night is young."

I spotted our waitress coming this way with the men's orders. I watched as Larry sipped his Cabernet Sauvignon.

Larry leered at the waitress, grabbing her arm. "This wine is almost as sweet as you. What time do you get off tonight, honey?"

"None of your business. Let go of me!" She jerked her arm from his grasp.

Taking advantage of the distraction, I sprang into action. As he cajoled her, trying to show off in front of Mike, I slipped strychnine into his expensive wine.

The waitress stomped off, and Larry had a good laugh with his buddy. I settled into my chair and waited.

Distracted, he downed the rest of his wine in a single

gulp. I watched as that chapter of my life closed and smiled at the knowledge he would leer no more.

THE OLD BRIDGE

Peter Becker held his lantern high. Even though his truck, which he'd left parked in the middle of the bridge, offered light, he didn't trust anything that ran on batteries.

"Ingrid, where are you?" he called.

Only silence answered through the thick fog.

He took a few careful steps, his joints popping.

"Ingrid! I'm sorry I yelled. Come home. Please." Every muscle in his body ached as he leaned over the bridge railing to peer into the black depths below. "I changed my mind. You may go to the moving pictures with young Frederick. But you must return home with me first."

He straightened stiffly. Hobbling back to his 1920 Oldsmobile Economy Truck, he continued calling for his lost daughter.

"I'm right here, Papa." Her voice was so soft that he barely heard her.

Peter rounded the truck to find his daughter sitting on the tailgate. Her short, beaded dress showed far more leg than he liked, but he knew he had to handle the situation with care. It was 1925, and times were changing.

"Climb inside the truck. This fog isn't good for you." His lips formed a smile that his heart didn't feel.

The teen leapt off the tailgate, skulking to the cab of the truck. Black fringes sewn to the bottom of her dress and sleeves swayed with her movement.

Peter put the truck in gear before speaking. "What are you doing out here on the bridge? Odd place to hide."

Her spine stiffened. "I wasn't hiding! I came here to meet Frederick, but he didn't come. I guess he changed his mind." With slumped shoulders, she leaned against the door, staring out the window.

"I see." Peter controlled the rage that washed through him. "Best to find out he's that type of man now rather than later."

She whispered, "I suppose."

It broke his heart to see his daughter so hurt. Once they arrived home, he made her some tea. Just what the doctor ordered for a broken heart.

"Why didn't he come? Do you think he wants to break up with me?" Her voice broke.

"Now, now. Don't cry. There are other young men in town. Better young men. What about Gabriel? He's an earnest boy with a good job. He will take over the bakery from his uncle one day. A life with him would be a life of comfort."

"I'm not going to date someone just because his uncle owns a bakery. I need a spark, and there is none with Gabriel. He's not nice. You might even say he's cruel in the things he does. He makes old ladies feel bad by telling them they're too slow and holding up the line at the bakery. He even teases stray dogs by waving a loaf of bread in the air and doesn't let them have any after they've jumped for it until their exhausted. No, I don't like Gabriel."

"But he would be a good provider. Frederick has no job or prospects. How would you live if you were to someday marry him?"

"I have that spark with Frederick. He makes me feel excited and happy. If we have love, the rest will follow.

Surely, there's something wrong. Where could he be?"

They both jumped at the stern knock on the door, Ingrid spilling what was left of her tea.

She ran to the door, throwing it open with all her strength. She visibly deflated when she saw the sheriff.

"Evenin' all." The lawman tipped his hat. "I need to have a word with the two of you."

Peter stood, ushering their guest into the living room. "What can we do for you, Sheriff?"

"Where were you both between 5 o'clock this evening and 8 o'clock?"

Ingrid ducked her head. "I snuck out. I went out to the old bridge to meet Frederick. Papa spent all evening looking for me."

Sheriff Tim Sanders nodded. "What about you, Peter? Were you out searching for her all evening?"

"Yes. We arrived home a short time ago. What's this about?" Peter asked.

"Can anyone else verify your whereabouts?"

They both shook their heads.

"I didn't want Papa to find me, so I stayed in the shadows until I gave up on my boyfriend coming."

Sheriff Sanders took a deep breath. "Frederick was found two miles downstream earlier this evening. It looks like he was stabbed and thrown in the river."

Ingrid whimpered. "Is he okay?"

"He's at the hospital. The doctor isn't sure he'll ever wake." He studied Peter for a moment. "You didn't want him dating Ingrid, did you?"

Peter's spine stiffened. "You think I tried to kill him? I'm not that sort of man. Ingrid can do better, sure. I'd prefer to see her with Gabriel from the bakery, a fine man with a steady job, but I don't wish Frederick ill."

"Papa could never hurt anyone! He's the kindest man in the entire state of Missouri." Tears flowed unabated down her cheeks.

Peter patted his daughter's hand. "He's just doing his job." Turning to the sheriff, he said, "I never harmed the boy."

She turned her tear-streaked face to the sheriff. "I love Frederick. You're here asking us questions when the person who hurt him is walking around free as a bird. Shouldn't you be out looking for him?"

"I'm sorry. I need to obtain statements from everyone close to him. I'm not accusing you or your papa of anything." After a few more questions, the lawman left.

"He can't die. I love him, Papa." The teen's shoulders shook with her sobs.

Turning to his beloved daughter, Peter said, "Get in the truck. We're going to the hospital."

At the front desk, they were directed to a large room filled with patients a few feet apart. They spotted Frederick right away.

Ingrid hurried to his side, lifting his hand. "I'm here, honey. Please be okay. I love you. Can you hear me? Wake up!"

Peter approached, his hat in his hand. "My boy, you need to wake up now. Ingrid's worried sick."

Sheriff Sanders sauntered in, his lips tightening as his gaze fell on them. "What are you two doing here?"

Glaring at the lawman, Ingrid gripped her love's hand tighter. "We didn't do this! We came to show him our love."

Frederick twitched, opening one eye. Seeing Peter, he tried to sit up.

The girl gently pushed him back into the pillow. "Just lie back. You don't want to hurt yourself more."

A tear escaped the young man's eye as he regarded Peter. "I'm sorry, sir. I shouldn't have let Ingrid go to the bridge. He could have gotten her, too."

"Who? Who did this?" the sheriff asked.

He turned his terrified gaze to the lawman. "Gabriel, the

baker."

    "Why would he do that?" the sheriff asked.

    "He told me it was fun."

J.C. FIELDS

J.C. Fields is a multi-award-winning and Amazon best-selling author. His Sean Kruger Series and The Michael Wolfe Saga have been awarded numerous gold, silver and bronze medals in the Reader's Favorite International Book Awards contest. In March of 2020, his book, *A Lone Wolf* became a #1 Best Selling Audiobook. The second book in the series, *The Last Insurgent*, gained Amazon's #1 New Release status in January 2021.

As one of the featured authors on the highly successful YouTube podcast, *Fear From the Heartland*, hosted by Paul J. McSorley, he offers a variety of original short stories penned specifically for its listeners.

He lives with his wife, Connie, in Southwest Missouri.

THE ALPHA TO OMEGA AFFAIR

Author Note: The story occurs five years before The Fugitive's Trail

FBI Agent Kruger shook hands with the CEO of Alpha to Omega, Burt Norman.

"What can I do for you today, Agent Kruger?"

Taking in the grandeur of the man's office, Kruger said, "I understand you've had seven associates murdered over the past two years."

Alpha to Omega Consulting, LLC, described their services as helping clients manage their employee's needs from the beginning to the end of employment. They were a large human resource firm that contracted with companies too small to have their own HR department. Their headquarters in Chicago occupied floors twenty through twenty-seven of the Willis Tower.

Raising an eyebrow, Norman said, "Unfortunately, yes. Why is this of any concern to the FBI?"

"The Ohio Attorney General asked us to investigate the matter. Two of the murders occurred in his state. And since both gentlemen worked for your company. I decided to start here."

"I see."

Kruger consulted his notes. "Why send only one person to a client company?"

"As a rule, we only send one associate to handle a company's personnel issues. Cheaper for our client companies."

"And for Alpha to Omega?"

Norman frowned but did not respond.

"Mr. Norman, what type of companies do you deal with?"

"As a rule, ones with fewer than a hundred employees."

"What kind of industries?"

"Mostly manufacturers."

"All you do is contract their HR needs, correct?"

A nod from Norman.

Kruger tilted his head. "How often do you send an associate to do mass lay-offs?"

"I beg your pardon."

"If a company needs to lay off most of its employees, they usually hire an outside firm to do so. How often is your company asked to provide those services?"

Norman's eyes flicked between Kruger and his desktop. He remained silent for a few moments. "It's about twenty-five percent of our annual revenue. We only provide that service to companies that do not use our full-service contract and have their own HR department."

"Why?"

"It keeps their HR personnel from being blamed by the surviving employees."

"How many of the murders occurred during those types of services?"

Taking a deep breath, Norman closed his eyes. "All of them."

"And you chose not to reveal this fact until now?"

A slow nod came from the CEO.

Kruger stood. "I'll need access to your files, Mr. Norman."

On the third day of cross-referencing the Alpha to Omega files, Kruger began to see a pattern emerge. A pattern with potential legal jeopardy for Alpha to Omega. He met with CEO Norman late on the third afternoon.

"Who assigns the associates sent to do the mass lay-offs, Mr. Norman?"

"That's the duty of the regional manager, Agent Kruger."

"They do it, or do they assign someone?"

"They do, company policy."

"I see."

Norman narrowed his eyes. "What are you implying, Agent Kruger?"

"I'm not implying anything. I'm following a possible lead."

"No, you're implying someone inside this company is responsible for the deaths?"

With a sly smile, Kruger appraised the now indignant CEO. "I didn't say that, Mr. Norman. You did. I merely asked who made the assignments."

The redness in Norman's face intensified, as did the pace of his breathing. Finally, he said, "Libby Carter. She's the head of our HR department. She is also the individual who determines who within the company has the skill sets to handle these types of assignments."

"I will need to interview her."

"When?"

"Now would be a good time."

"Thank you for taking the time to meet with me, Ms. Carter." Kruger sat at the head of a long conference table in a room next to the CEO's office.

"I didn't think I had a choice, Agent Kruger."

"Would you prefer to have an attorney present?"

"Am I a suspect?"

Tilting his head, the special agent said, "Should you be?"

She shook her head.

"Do you want an attorney?"

"No." She paused. "I can't afford one."

This statement gave Kruger pause. He made a note and asked, "Burt Norman indicated you are the head of the company's HR department."

"Yes."

"Do you assign the individuals who will be heading out into the field?"

She shook her head, "What gave you that idea?"

"I'm trying to determine how the company serves your clients."

"With regional managers."

"Can you explain how that works?"

"I would have assumed Mr. Norman would have explained."

"Indulge me, please."

"When Alpha to Omega sign a client in, let's say, Wichita, Kansas, we also hire a regional rep to handle the business. That individual is then assigned to recruit other companies to utilize our services within that geographical area."

"Is Regional Manager responsible for all businesses within an area?"

"Yes. If they grow their client list, we authorize them to hire staff to help with the day-to-day needs."

Kruger nodded. "So, if a company contracts with this regional manager to help lay off employees, who does he send in?"

"The regional manager is responsible for that duty."

Staying silent, Kruger made a note. He then looked up. "What's your turnover rate?"

"In what department?"

"Regional Managers."

"Not very high. Most of them have six-figure incomes."

"Okay, interesting. What happens when one retires or dies?"

"Other regional managers bid on their territories."

Kruger raised an eyebrow. "What do you mean bid?"

"They can offer to manage the clients within that geographical area for a smaller percentage of the revenue generated."

He sat back in his chair. "So, each regional manager is a business unit within itself?"

"Basically. They have to adhere to company standards, but in a sense, they are independent."

"Thank you, Ms. Carter."

That night in his hotel room, Kruger studied the files given to him by the CEO. One group of facts was absent, financial records. He also reviewed the files of the seven regional managers who had been killed. He then searched on Google and when he found the right page, a small smile came to his lips. He checked the time and made a phone call.

The Next Afternoon

Five FBI agents from the Chicago Field Office accompanied Kruger as they entered the offices of Alpha to

Omega Consulting, LLC. The receptionist tried to stop them as they blew past her desk, heading for the room Kruger knew the CEO occupied. The door was open and Burt Norman could be seen at his desk consulting with two associates. Those men turned as the group of six FBI agents, all dressed in suits, entered the space.

Norman frowned and said, "What is the meaning of this intrusion?"

Kruger handed the man a folded document. "We are subpoenaing your financial records, Mr. Norman."

The CEO opened the page and skimmed the words. "Those are confidential records. You can't have them."

Pointing to the page, Kruger smiled. "That was signed by a federal judge this morning, and it says we can." He turned to his associates. "Gentlemen, please proceed as we discussed."

As the other agents filed out of the room, Burt Norman turned to Kruger. "You could have asked for them."

"Would you have given me all the files?"

The CEO stared at the FBI agent for a few moments and then shook his head.

"That's the reason for the subpoena. What are we going to find, Mr. Norman?"

"I believe it's time for me to contact an attorney."

"Wise idea, sir."

Illinois Attorney General Josh Barnes looked over the files lying on his desk. "What am I looking at, Sean?"

Pointing to the flow chart Kruger had prepared from the financial records, he said, "Alpha to Omega Consulting have seven offices in Ohio, Illinois, Michigan, Indiana and Wisconsin. Ohio and Michigan have two, whereas the rest only have one. Those states have a large population of small manufacturers, ninety percent with fewer than one hundred employees."

"Okay, why's that important?"

"Alpha to Omega has a thriving business in each of those states. The commissions paid to the regional managers in those states alone amounted to over thirty million dollars a year."

"A substantial amount. Go on."

"If a regional manager leaves the company or dies, that region can be awarded to another regional manager who could bid with a lower commission. Substantially lower in this case."

Barnes frowned. "You're kidding."

"Nope. All seven of the regional managers who were killed earned the highest commissions of any others throughout the other states where Alpha does business. The regional managers who took those regions over are receiving a fraction of the compensation the previous managers received."

"So, who killed the original managers?"

"I think there are only two individuals who know."

"Burt Norman?"

"He's one of them."

"Who's the other."

"Libby Carter."

"Can you prove it?"

"Without a doubt. As long as I can offer her a deal."

"What do you have in mind?"

Kruger told him.

◆ ◆ ◆

"Thank you for meeting me away from your office, Ms. Carter." The two were in a Starbucks one block from the Willis Building.

"Honestly, Agent Kruger, I don't know what else I can tell you."

"Why did you ask if you needed an attorney the last time we met?"

She stared at the FBI agent for a long time. Her lip quivered and she diverted her eyes to the coffee cup in her hand. "I was nervous."

"To be expected. But you didn't seem nervous. In fact, you were quite confident. You asked matter-of-factly, like you asked the question on a daily basis. Why is that Ms. Carter?"

"I think I do need an attorney."

"Why, Ms. Carter?"

She stood. "I feel entrapped by your insinuations."

"I haven't insinuated anything, Ms. Carter. I'm simply asking questions."

The woman stared at him but did not move.

"Why don't you sit down, Ms. Carter, and I'll tell you a story."

She sat, but kept her purse in her lap and did not glance at Kruger.

He told her what he knew. When he finished, she continued to sit there and stare out the window next to their table.

"Burt can be a charming man when he wants to be. He told me all I had to do was get the employee records for the individuals to be laid off and I could expect a nice bonus."

"How much?"

She smiled and looked at the FBI agent. "When my husband died several years ago, he left me with nothing but bills. I didn't know he had a gambling problem. Mr. Norman paid them off for me."

"What did you have to do for the bonus?"

"Find out if any of the employee's being laid off had a criminal record."

"Did you?"

She nodded.

"And?"

"That was all, nothing else."

"So, once he knew who had a criminal record, he contacted them and made them a deal What kind of deal?"

"If they killed the man who laid them off, they'd get a ticket to anywhere in the country, plus ten thousand dollars."

"Seven men took him up on the offer?"

She nodded again.

"Ms. Carter, you could be considered an accomplice to murder."

"I know."

"Will you be willing to testify against Burt Norman?"

She looked at him with narrowed eyes. "Only if I can get a deal."

"It's your lucky day."

The arrest of Burt Norman occurred two days later. Agents from the Chicago Field Office did the honors while Kruger watched. The Special Agent in Charge of Chicago, Bob Simmons, stood next to him.

"How solid is our case against Norman?"

"Granite."

A small frown appeared on the man's face. "Based only on the Carter woman's testimony?"

"Nope."

Simmons chuckled. "What else do you have up your sleeve, Sean?"

"The written statement from each of the men he hired to kill the regional managers."

If you enjoyed this short Sean Kruger story, check out J.C. Fields' full-length novels featuring FBI Profiler Sean Kruger at www.jcfieldsbooks.com

THE TELLTALE TRUNK

Betsy, our 911 dispatcher, laid the While-You-Were-Out note on my desk. I read it and looked up at her. "Yuck."

She nodded. "Paul, she was hysterical and incoherent. I needed to slow her down several times just to figure out what she was saying."

Looking at the note one more time, I opened my desk drawer and lifted my Glock 21 out and placed it in the holster on my right hip. My old worn Stetson was on a hook behind the door. I placed it on my head as I left the office.

"They're in there." Cathy Stovall pointed at the storage room.

The room was chaotic. Dust-coated cobwebs clung to every sharp angle. Pictures, trunks, dishes, broken chairs, books, and assorted junk were strewn. The room smelled old and reminded me of a scene from Oscar Wilde's *The Picture of Dorian Gray*.

"Which one?"

Cathy stood outside, one hand covering her mouth and

the other pointing at one of the trunks on the back wall. "The brown one."

I stared in the direction her finger indicated and tipped my hat back on my head. "They're all brown. Which brown one?"

"Top."

I nodded and moved several pictures and a wicker basket to get to the trunk. It wasn't heavy and I placed it in the only open space I could find on the dirty floor. Wiping my dusty hands on my jeans, I turned my back to Cathy and kneeled to examine the broken lock. "Was the lock like this before you opened it?"

"Yes, sir."

A pungent odor emanated from the trunk. I took a deep breath and held it. Lifting the lid, I exhaled sharply and stood up. Three human skulls with patchy decaying skin and hair, their eye sockets empty, stared up at me. I reached for my cell phone.

"Is this the first time you've been in your aunt's storage room?"

Her head bobbed up and down.

"Did you know it was even there?"

The non-talkative Cathy Stovall shook her head sideways.

We were sitting at a wooden table in the late Kathleen Stovall's kitchen. "Who owns the house?"

"According to the will, I do." Finally, words from her mouth.

"Cathy, I can't help if you don't provide details."

"She was a bit strange, and we weren't close. This is the first time I've been here. I'm her only surviving relative."

Cathy is a petite woman in her mid-forties with short brown hair. Her pretty face was streaked with dust and tears. "I see. Who contacted you about her death?"

She reached into her jean pocket, retrieved a crumbled business card and handed it to me. The talkative phase apparently over.

I stared at the card. "May I keep this?"

She nodded.

◆

"Who handled the estate?"

Ted Nelson was in his late seventies and operated a two-person law office. "I wrote the will, and my secretary handled the details, Sheriff Osborne. We're a small firm."

"It's a small county."

Nelson nodded.

"When did the husband die?"

"Which one?"

"I beg your pardon?"

"There were three. She never took any of their last names."

"Divorced?"

Nelson nodded. "Reason was abandonment."

"You're kidding?"

"Nope."

"How long ago?

"Last one left twenty years ago."

"Do you know what happened?"

"All three couldn't put up with her. They just disappeared and never came back."

I leaned back in my chair. "Uh, oh."

"What?"

◆

"Crime lab."

I was on my cell phone with the regional crime lab while

I drove to the nursing home.

"This is Bishop County, Sheriff Paul Osborne. Have you guys examined the skulls found at the Stovall House?"

"Yeah."

"Are they real?"

"Yeah."

"How old?"

"Old."

I rolled my eyes. "Details, son."

"Sheriff, they haven't been here long enough to determine, probably at least twenty years or more."

I parked the Tahoe in front of the Bishop County Manor. The facility was the last home of Kathleen Stovall before her passing. The nice lady at the reception desk directed me to the right resident.

"So, you were the last roommate of Kathleen Stovall?"

"First and last." Mae Curtis sat in a wheelchair in the visitor's lounge. She was in her nineties, frail, and bent over like a question mark, but alert and feisty.

"I'm sorry—first and last?"

"Yup. She couldn't get along with anyone, especially men. She ended up in a room by herself with only unconscious residences knocking on death's door as roommates."

I suppressed a smile. "What was she like?"

"Mean, foul-mouthed and cantankerous. Didn't have a nice word for anyone."

"When you were roommates, did she ever talk about her husbands?"

Mae stared at me like I possessed a third eye. "She didn't like men. Thought they were the scourge of womankind. The witch never mentioned being married."

I nodded. "Three times."

"Huh…"

"She never mentioned them?"

Mae shook her head. "Not to me."

I sat back in the Pine-Sol-smelling lounge chair across from her. "Do you know of anyone here who talked to her?"

She studied the pattern in her lap blanket. I let her think. Finally, she looked up. "The little volunteer who pushes us to meals was always talking to Kathleen. Maybe she can help you."

Becky Cole was eighteen and volunteered at the Manor through her church.

"She was always nice to me, constantly talking about her life."

Finally, someone who might shed light on Kathleen Stovall. "Did she mention her husbands?"

"Yes, she told me never to get married and how horrible it was to live with a man."

"You believed her?"

Becky laughed, "Of course not. I like boys."

"Did she say what happened to them?"

"No, she just told me they left."

"What else did she tell you about herself?"

"She used to brag about being a set designer for haunted houses in Kansas City."

"A set designer?"

"Yes, she was really proud of her props. Especially the Halloween ones."

I dreaded the answer to my next question. "Did she mention any skulls?"

"She sure did. They were her pride and joy. Very life like, she told me."

"How many did she have?"

"Three, just the three."

"Did she mention where she kept them?"

"Yes, sir. She told me all of her props were still in storage at her house."

"Did she mention where she kept the skulls?"

"Yes, a brown trunk with a broken lock."

THE LAUNDROMAT

Jonny Kendrick took the last drag on a cigarette and tossed it toward the street. He leaned against a traffic light pole and pointed at the building across the street. "I think we should rob that laundromat."

Billy Porter, an overweight ex-high school wrestler, stared at the scrawny man next to him. "What are you? Stupid. I ain't robbing no laundromat. What're we gonna do with all those quarters, man?"

"We turn them into cash, man. It's the perfect crime."

"Geez, are you a moron, or has your bad breath been eatin' a hole in your brain? How's it the perfect crime?"

"Ya, see, they got all these quarters in there, man. Quarters can't be marked like dollar bills. We steal em, take em to a Walmart and use one of those machines that turn quarters into dollar bills. Walla, you've laundered your money, so to speak." He chuckled at his own joke.

"Oh, my, gawd, Jonny, what's wrong with you? Did your mama drop you on your head as a kid? That's the dumbest idea I've ever heard."

Kendrick lit another cigarette and inhaled deeply. As he blew out smoke, he smiled. "It's not a dumb idea, Billy. It makes sense. I'm telling ya it's the perfect crime."

As he stepped off the curb, Porter grabbed his arm.

"Hold on, man. You can't just dash in there and demand quarters. Ya gotta case the joint. See who's there. Might be a cop's washin' his underwear or something. Then, what've ya got? A quick trip to jail."

Taking another long drag on his cigarette, Kendrick stared forlornly at the business across the street. As he blew smoke through his nose, he nodded. "Yeah, ya got a point."

Porter grew serious. "Let's go in and see what we're up against."

"Good idea, let's do it."

After they crossed the busy avenue and stood looking at the building, a black and white police car screamed past with sirens blaring and light bar flashing reds and blues.

Kendrick jumped and stared at the receding vehicle. "Bad omen, Billy."

"Nah, we ain't done nuthin, yet. We go in and we check it out."

Taking the lead, Porter entered the building and surveyed the two dozen washing machines. He noticed an equal number of dryers.

Kendrick followed close behind the larger man and noticed the slots on the coin acceptors were not round. The shape looked more like a pentagon than a circle. He mumbled, "What the heck?" The smaller of the two men scratched his two-week-old patchy beard. "Those don't look like quarters, Billy."

"No, they don't. I'll ask that lady over there." Porter took off toward a gray-haired woman folding towels at an eight-foot-long table. When he got there, she turned and gave him a *what-the-heck-do-you-want* stare.

"Yeah?"

"My quarters don't fit the machines. What the hell am I supposed to use on these things?"

She pointed to a sign above the table where she worked.

Billy looked up and saw, FOR YOUR SAFETY THIS IS A COIN-FREE OPERATION. USE YOUR DEBIT OR

CREDIT CARD TO BUY TOKENS.

He mumbled, "Thanks," and walked back to Kendrick. As they headed out the door, he said, "Real bright idea Einstein, they don't use quarters anymore."

KEN GARDNER

Ken Gardner didn't begin writing until he was thirty. After graduating with his MFA in creative writing from the University of Southern Maine in 2018, he began working on his books. After recovering from COVID-19 in November 2020, he decided it was time to get serious about publishing.

Since then, Ken is an award-winning writer of short stories. His first book, *Blood Storm*, launched in 2022. It is a Christian fiction murder mystery that delves into the time period his father had been studying for decades, the Tribulation as described in John's Revelation and other prophetic texts in the Bible.

Ken lives in southwest Missouri with his wife, Shelly, son, Hunter, and German Shepherd, Tank. Sports are a point of great distraction, especially, the St. Louis Cardinals, college football, and the NFL draft.

THE CEDAR CHEST

The vacant look in Grandpa's soft green eyes showed a man imprisoned in his own mind without parole or pardon. The temporary furloughs, few and far between, became more so in the last two years. The hardest part came from reducing his possessions to fit his memory care room that only had a bathroom, a small closet, and little else. Since the rest of the family lived out of state, I was the obvious choice for the job because I worked at the Missouri State Highway Patrol Crime Laboratory at Jordan Valley Community Health Center in Springfield, Missouri as a forensic DNA analyst.

The maintenance workers of the small Missouri nursing home had already moved his bed, nightstand, dresser, and television, so I needed to go through the rest of his possessions. It took all morning to separate and box the clothes, memorabilia, and knick-knacks. I sat in front of the only thing left, the cedar chest he used as a coffee table.

The top layers were blankets and a couple of dresses in plastic vacuum clothes bags that he must have saved after Grandma died. Brownish stains on the dresses obviously came from her famous chocolate cupcakes. She loved to bake but was a little messy. She always said that bad cooks kept clean clothes.

The rest of the contents were pictures from the years they were together. Grandma was trim and tall with the same red hair I have. Grandpa had broad shoulders and stood a few inches taller with dark wavy hair. A truly handsome couple. He hid his devastation behind unemotional eyes when the doctor gave her diagnosis of metastatic breast cancer at fifty-two, but he retreated deeper within himself when she died eight months later. He never remarried, let alone dated.

After clearing the last of the pictures, I noticed a small hole near the center of the chest. I put my finger in it and noticed that it didn't touch the shag carpet below. Bending my finger and pulling, the false bottom easily popped up. The only things underneath were five small Ziplock bags that had locks of auburn hair that matched Grandma's. When Alzheimer's took over, he began hiding things everywhere for reasons only known to him. Wondering if they were hers or mine, I took them with me to the lab.

The locks I found were perfect to run diagnostics on some of my machines since the hair roots were intact. The DNA should've matched Grandma's or mine because we were in the system. Grandma let me practice on her during my training, a requirement of my job.

The next day, I looked at the results with silent shock. None of the samples matched Grandma's or my DNA. After putting them in NDIS (The National DNA Index System), waiting a few hours, and reading the results, my tears landed on the keyboard. Five missing women reports filled the screen. Each woman was the spitting image of Grandma. All missing and feared dead after Grandma had passed.

SHARON KIZZIAH-HOLMES

Sharon Kizziah-Holmes has been an indie-author since 2002 and is well versed in the self-publishing industry. She is the co-founder and co-owner of Paperback Press LLC., with imprints Paperback Press, Kids Book Press, Indie Pub Press and Audio Book Press.

She has served as publishing coordinator to over two-hundred authors, assisted in publishing five hundred plus books for writers in the US and abroad. Several have become bestselling, self-published authors.

A board member of Ozarks Creative Writers Conference, Co-Chair of Between the Pages Writers Con and President of Ozarks Romance authors, Sharon also remains active in many other writers' groups.

If you need guidance or want to know about self-publishing, take advantage of her expertise. She can answer your questions.

Sharon loves to help writers of all genres realize their publishing dream.

GUILTY UNTIL PROVEN INNOCENT

"**I**f only what was said could be taken back!"

"What's done is done. Now we have to find out the truth."

Sarah Van Jones sat at the table in her mother, Patricia's kitchen. "The truth is, I know about his 'secret meeting' with *her*."

"You have to keep positive thoughts."

Positive thoughts? She wanted to wring the hussy's beautiful neck! "Easy for you to say. It's not your husband, Mom." She shouldn't have said that. Her father passed away a few years ago from an unknown cause. At least *her husband was alive* even if he was a cheat.

"There's has to be a logical explanation for the meetings."

"Oh, there's a logical reason all right. It's spelled S.E.X. Something we haven't had in a while. He says he loves me. Now I know that's bullshit."

Her hand shook when she picked up her cup of coffee. She'd made up her mind "I'm going to flat out ask that bastard if he's boinkin' her."

Her mother snickered. "Boinking?"

She almost laughed herself. If she wasn't so hurt... mad... she would. "You know what I mean."

"Yes, I do. There are other ways to find out." Patricia tapped her fingers on the table.

"I could hire a private investigator."

"If it's not true, you don't want to taint things with accusations." Patricia sat back in her chair. "This all might be a big misunderstanding. Who told you about this?"

Sarah shook her head "I don't know. The voice sounded like there was some device attached to the line making it distorted. I couldn't tell if it was a man or a woman."

"Maybe they dialed the wrong person. It could have been for someone else. Do you still have the number on your phone?"

"The caller ID said it was private, so no." Tears welled in her eyes, and she met her mother's gaze. "Mom, what if Jay is cheating on me?"

When she looked at her mother there was a strange sparkle of mischief in her eyes. What was on her mind? "Mom? What are you thinking?" Usually, when the older woman got that look in her eye it meant trouble.

"We're going to conduct an investigation. *If* that man of yours is cheating, I know exactly how to handle it."

"Are you going to let me in on it?"

"We'll have our own 'secret meeting' with one or both of them."

The smile, lifted on Patricia Marshall's face, creeped Sarah out. She'd always known her mom was weird, but this was something she'd never seen.

"You know what, Mom. I think I'll let you handle it." If the woman thought she could figure it all out, more power to her.

◆━◆━◆

Sarah Van Jones' pulse beat in her temples as she took the witness stand. She placed her left hand on the Bible, lifted her right, and looked the court recorder in the eye.

She shivered at the man's words. How could this have happened? She was innocent. The anticipation of what could happen made her tremble inside while trying to keep her cool on the outside.

The reporter asked, "Mrs. Van Jones, do you swear to tell the truth, the whole truth and nothing but the truth, so help you God?"

"I solemnly swear to tell the truth, the whole truth and nothing but the truth, so help me God."

The prosecuting attorney stepped up to the stand and studied her for a few moments before he spoke. Her mom's hand trembled slightly when she brushed some hair away from her face. How could she convince them?

"Mrs. Van Jones, is it true you were at 444 Bingham Rd. the night of the incident?"

"Yes, that's my home, of course, I was there."

"Did you go anywhere that evening? Say…between 5:00 p.m. and 6:30 p.m."

She couldn't stop fidgeting. "Why, no, sir, I didn't."

Nodding his head, the prosecutor furrowed his brow. "What would you say if we told you we have video footage of you entering the dentist's office that evening around 5:37 p.m?"

"I would say it wasn't me. I stayed home that night."

"I see. So, you're telling me someone who looked like you, maybe even disguised as you, could be the person in the video?" He turned away from Sarah.

"How would I know? But I can tell you it… Was. Not. Me." When he looked toward her again, his glare made her breath catch in her throat.

"But you *were* there, weren't you? You *are* the one who killed your husband and Mrs. Wingo aren't you? Admit it, Mrs. Van Jones, you're the murderer!"

He kept yelling. She was so confused. She forced herself to breathe and placed her hands over her ears to make it all go away. "No! No, I didn't!" she yelled back.

"You knew your husband was secretly meeting her at her office after hours, didn't you?"

"Yes, but—"

"But! What you didn't know is he was actually doing an apprenticeship with Dr. Wingo to become a dental technician. He wanted to surprise you with his new career. Mr. Wingo knew all about the training meetings. However, you didn't ask your husband before you murdered him, did you? You found out, thought they were lovers and killed them! Didn't you, Mrs. Van Jones."

Sobs wracked her body. Why was this happening? "No." She whispered.

"Stop!"

Sarah tried to blink back her tears when she heard her mother's voice. What was she doing? She wiped her face with the back of her hand, unable to comprehend the words her mother said.

"I did it! I killed him *and* the woman. Just like I killed my husband all those years ago!"

If someone's heart could stop all at once, Sarah feared hers would. Why was her mother saying that? Surely she–.

"We thought they were having an affair. It broke my daughter's heart and I couldn't stand for it! No one ever found my husband's killer. I thought I could get away with it again." Tears flowed freely down her cheeks. She met Sarah's gaze. "But I didn't. And I refuse to let my daughter take the blame."

The prosecutor stepped forward. "But they weren't having an affair at those 'secret meetings', were they, Mrs. Marshall?"

If looks could kill, the prosecutor would have dropped dead. Sarah couldn't believe what her mother said next.

"How the hell was I supposed to know?!"

CURIOSITY DIDN'T KILL THE CAT

Julie heard a muffled cry, a thud, then silence. A noise in the hallway of her apartment building came next. Not just a noise, but someone walking. Something about the sounds made her uneasy. What was going on?

The power outage didn't settle her nerves, but she was compelled to investigate. No, whatever it was, she didn't want to get involved. She settled back in her chair and watched the flickering wick of the candle on the end table.

It was a stupid thing to do at this time of night, even if the lights were on, but curiosity got the best of her. She stood, candle in hand, and made her way to the door. Why was she doing this? Was she crazy? Stepping cautiously, she felt something underfoot.

"Rreeoooww!"

Her heart jumped to her throat, and she almost dropped the small torch she held. "Damn, Bartley, you scared the crap out of me. Are you okay?" She reached down and ran her hand down the cat's back. It purred and cuddled against her. "I guess you are." But was she? She straightened and inhaled deeply, which did little to calm her, but she had to push forward. No, she didn't have to, she wanted to. "Now, get out of the way. I need to see who's lurking in the hallway."

She pushed the feline aside and reached for the deadbolt. The lights flickered on for a scant second, then off again. On. Off. She held her breath, hoping the power would be restored. She waited. Nothing.

The footsteps of whoever was outside her apartment grew fainter by the moment. They would take the stairs shortly. She had to hurry. It was now or never. The bolt lock clicked when she turned it. She swallowed hard and reached for the knob. It was cool to the touch, and she shivered. Was it the coolness that made her react that way, or a sixth since she was about to open her world to danger?

Slowly she pulled the door ajar and stared into the darkness of the corridor. Her pulse pounded in her temple. Why was she so frightened? This was ridiculous. She straightened her spine and peered out. Looking to her right she saw nothing, but when she glanced to her left, a tall man in a trench coat made his way up the stairs. He held a flashlight in his left hand as he ascended.

He paused. Had he heard her door open? The flashlight illuminated something in his right hand. A knife! He turned and shined the light directly into her eyes, blinding her momentarily.

The power came on and the lights lit the hallway. He stared straight at her, his face etched in her memory. She glanced down. Drops of blood marked the floor outside her door, then she saw the body.

Before she could close the door, he was in front of her. A sharp pain stabbed in her chest and her world went black.

MURDER AT THE READ

"**W**hat the hell?"

I glanced at Michael. He frowned and stared at the ceiling of our motel room. Following his gaze, I spotted... blood spatter?

An eerie feeling came over me, and a shiver ran down my spine. Had someone died in this room? The lump in my throat went down hard. "My gawd, Mike, do you think someone was killed here?"

A cold, unnatural draft hit me when he got out of bed to study the spatter. At six-foot-three inches tall, he could touch the eight-foot-high ceiling easily, but being a police officer, he knew that might compromise a murder scene.

The wail of agony from another room was piercing. Compelled to dress, I jumped out of bed as Michael reached for his jeans. A deep moaning sound then another wail penetrated the walls. "

"I'll go see what's happening."

"No, please leave it to the local authorities."

Every time he walked out the door for his shift on the Kansas City Police Department, I wondered if he'd walk back through. This was supposed to be our vacation. In Chattanooga we shouldn't have to deal with crime. Now this? Why?

He reached into his travel bag and pulled out the Glock 22 he carried at work. "You know I can't stand by to let someone get hurt. I have to see what's going on. You stay here and call 911."

Loaded clip in hand, he slammed it into his weapon and pulled back the slide, then released it to put a round into the chamber. It was a sound I had heard hundreds of times, but it always made me cringe. I knew that a single bullet could kill someone in an instant. I hated the knowledge, but I loved my man, and he loved his job, so it was something I had to learn to live with.

My cell phone was cold to the touch when I picked it up. It felt like it had been in the fridge. I shivered once again. Something wasn't right. I heard Michael's voice.

"Here, keep this handy just in case you need it."

I didn't know he'd packed my Smith & Wesson .38 special revolver. Early in our marriage he insisted I get my conceal carry license, so I took the classes and learned how to shoot.

It didn't make me like carrying *or* like knowing I might be forced to kill someone someday. Initially I didn't carry all the time, but with things like they are in the world today, I realized it made me feel safer when I was out in public by myself. However, I never thought about bringing it on vacation. Damn.

Arm extended, Glock in hand, Michael opened the door and in true police fashion cased the hallway before he put both hands on the grip and with arms in front of him, stepped out of the room.

"911, what is your emergency?"

I was freezing and when I spoke, my breath coming out like a small misty cloud on a cold winter night. I glanced around but couldn't see the source of the chill in the air.

"Hello? What is your emergency?"

The dispatcher's voice drew my attention and made me

focus on why I had called. "My husband and I heard a scream, of sorts, from down the hall."

"What is your location, ma'am?"

"The Read House Hotel."

"I see."

Was that humor I heard in the woman's voice? Did she think someone possibly being murdered or hurt in some way was funny? "Are you going to send a patrol car? My husband is a policeman in Kansas City and he's gone to see if he can help until someone gets here."

"Yes, ma'am, we'll send a patrolman, but I have to tell you, we get these calls from that location about once a week. The Read House is haunted by the ghost of Annalisa Netherly."

Realizing I was holding my breath, I let it out slowly. The cloud of mist was once again prevalent on the moisture of my breath. "Haunted?"

"Yes, ma'am. I don't think you have anything to worry about, but our officer is on site, so he'll check it out.

Now I felt a presence in the room with me, then I heard our room door open, but no one was there. I couldn't tell if I was trembling or shivering from the cold. "Michael?"

I stood and approached the opened door, which held an invitation that beckoned me into the hallway. Men's voices came from another area of the hall. Cautious of my surroundings, I held my .38 and stepped out. Again, my breath a puff of vapor on the air.

To my left I heard a noise. I raised my revolver and pointed it in that direction. A white apparition stood at the end of the hallway in front of a strange mirror, dressed in clothes from the 1800s. She motioned me to come toward her.

My heart raced as I glanced over my shoulder and called, "Michael!" When I turned back the woman was gone. Mike and the police officer were by my side and my husband put his arm around my waist.

"What happened? You're freezing."

"I saw a ghost."

"Honey, no you didn't. There is no such thing."

The officer stepped forward. "Are you folks in room 311."

Michael looked at the man. "Yes, we are."

"That explains all of this."

"What are you talking about?" Mike asked.

"In the 1800s, Annalisa Netherly was caught with another man by her husband. In a rage, he killed her. Now she takes it out on unsuspecting guests. Did you see blood spatter on the ceiling?"

I nodded and so did Michael. Had we really witnessed a haunting?

"That's a sure sign she's going to show up. Come with me."

He led the way back to our room. When I looked up, the spatter was gone, but a disturbing laugh echoed through the walls.

It was apparent Annalisa was enjoying the events of the evening. I, however, was angry. Whispering under my breath, I hoped she would hear me, "Bitch."

SOCIAL MEDIA CONFESSION

"What the hell you doing now?"

Maryanne didn't like her husband's tone. "I'm trying to get some answers. No one vanishes off the face of the earth, never to be found again. And you don't have to cuss, Kent."

"For gawd sake, are you still hung up on that lady's disappearance? What about those three women that went missing in Springfield, Missouri? They've never been found...It happens." He paused. "And you think you're going to find what you need on the internet?"

"You never know. Sunshine Freemont has a Facebook page, a twitter account, Instagram and all that stuff. Surely she would post something, somewhere. I'm friends with her on all of those platforms."

Kent cleared his throat. "Y-you are?"

"Yes, I have been for quite some time." She glanced at him. "Why are you fidgeting? Do you know something I don't?"

"No, I just need some coffee, that's all." He started for the kitchen.

Maryanne had noticed he'd been nervous the last few weeks. She watched him walk away. He looked thinner, and his pajama bottoms didn't fit quite right. Was he sick?

She'd make a point to talk to him about it later. Now she wanted to get back to her research. She had never 'social media' stalked anyone before, but maybe she could find useful information by doing just that.

On Instagram, she looked through all of Sunshine's pictures. The last post was the day before she went missing. "Nothing interesting here." It was on to Facebook. She read all of Sunshine's posts for the two weeks before she disappeared. Surely there was something, but she was tired of looking at pictures of food and– "What the…"

The words on a post from over a month ago drew her attention…

I seldom ever air my 'dirty laundry' as some call it, on social media, but I have to get this off my chest. Please forgive me for what I'm about to tell you.

Most of you don't know I've been seeing someone, but I have. He told me today we couldn't see each other anymore. He's afraid his 'wife' will find out about us.

A married man you say? I know, I'm bad, having an affair with K, but I couldn't help myself. He is irresistible in my eyes. Funny, I don't even know K's last name, but I realize I love him. I can tell you this, I'm not going to let him go that easily. I'll fight to the death for his love. That's a promise.

Please don't hate me for loving a man that belongs to someone else. One good thing about this whole…sordid affair, is they don't have kids. I may be a home wrecker, but at least I'm not hurting any children.

Now that you know my dirty little secret, I'll wait to get slammed in your comments. If you're my true friend, I'd appreciate your good thoughts, prayers, mojo or whatever you might practice. This isn't going to be an easy battle.

Maryanne swallowed the lump in her throat. Kent had been so quiet when he stepped behind her, she didn't even know he was there until that very moment. Had he snuck up on her? Why?

Wait, Sunshine mentioned the first letter of her lover's name was K? Could that stand for Kent? No, it couldn't be. Yet he'd been staying late at work a lot. That is until the last couple of weeks. As a matter of fact, since Sunshine went missing, he'd been home every night.

Her heart sank. She couldn't let her imagination run away with her. First of all, he wouldn't have an affair, her husband loved her. Didn't he? And there was no way he could be involved in anything as evil as... murder. Could he?

Her heart threatened to stop beating when she slowly turned toward her husband. The look in his eyes was one she'd never seen before. It frightened her. "Kent? W-what are you doing?"

She saw the slightest movement of his arm and glanced down to see one of her silk scarves in his hand. His voice was low, raspy and wicked.

"I'm sorry you had to read that, my love. Now you and Sunshine will be more than social media friends. You'll be grave partners."

In a blink of an eye, the scarf was around her neck, squeezing her life away. Just before darkness overtook her, a faint sound rang out. The doorbell.

"Police! Open the door!"

VJ SCHULTZ

VJ Schultz resides in Springfield, Missouri, with husband, John and four cats. Inspiration for her writing comes from the interesting people of the region, the beautiful Ozarks Mountains and lakes, and God's wonderful prompts. She has short story anthologies on Amazon.com, including Death of Bigfoot & Other Tales.

THE MIGHTY OAK HAS FALLEN

The oak tree tattoo looked good, Jessie thought. Well, except for the red lightning bolt someone had slashed across the inked art.

But that desecration would never matter to the shirtless man sprawled face down on the ground by Jessie's feet. The knife sunk hilt deep into the tree on his back made sure of that.

Jessie shook his head. The evil of men had long ago ceased to amaze him. He preferred the company of dogs, cats, and other critters, having a gift for communing with them. He turned his attention to the half-grown mixed-breed dog huddled by the dead man. The dog was Jessie's mission at this crime scene.

"Poor boy," he whispered, then whistled softly and watched the dog's ears twitch. "Need a friend, young one?"

Jessie continued to speak calmly, sending thoughts of safety to the fear-filled canine while inching forward. Finally, he held out a hand. Although he hoped for a cautious sniff, the dog jumped into his arms, nearly knocking him over where he crouched. "Easy there, boy."

Running his hands over the pup, he found a small knife wound on the front leg. Petting and reassuring the animal, he fastened the leash he'd brought onto the dog's collar, read the name 'Sam', and removed a stub of chewed through rope. That item he handed over to a deputy.

Jessie, carrying Sam, paused by Sheriff Petree. Sam came to life, growled furiously, and struggled in Jessie's arms.

"Hey," Petree waved him away. "Get that mutt put up."

After depositing Sam in his van, Jessie returned to the officers standing at a distance from the body. Together they stood in silence for a moment watching the team collecting evidence.

"Any idea of what went down here? It sure wasn't an accident?" Jessie nodded toward the body.

"Looks like the mighty oak has fallen," Petree said.

Jessie watched the sheriff's mouth pucker to spit, then become a frown as he likely remembered about DNA and crime scenes.

"So you know the guy? You can't even see his face."

"A troublemaker. Guy's spent half his life in jail. No surprise he got himself killed. Makes a mess for me." Petree adjusted his hat.

"Any relatives that might want to take the dog?"

Pointing his chin at the deceased, Petree said, "Naw. His brothers are in prison where I put them. His parents are dead. Guess that mutt will end up in dog jail. Take him to the pound." Petree absently tugged his sleeve down, fingering a ragged edge on the otherwise pristine uniform.

"Don't you want to keep him as a witness or have him checked out?"

"Witness? You nuts? It's just a mutt."

"Well, he might have DNA or some such evidence on him. There's a cut on his leg."

Petree shrugged. "This isn't TV CSI. Heck, keep him if you want. Just don't bring him to me. Dogs and me don't get along." With that, Petree waved his hand. "Time for you to vacate, too. We got enough to do without being distracted."

Frowning, Jessie returned to his van. None of this felt right in his gut. Petree wasn't someone he'd dealt with before and he hoped he wouldn't have to again. Something about Petree made the back of Jessie's neck itch. Rather than drop Sam at the pound, he got out his cellphone and dialed a friend. "I've got a hurt pup I'd like you to look at; poor fellow was involved in a crime scene. And I'd like him checked for possible evidence."

Susan McAdams met him at the door of her vet's office. He carried Sam into an exam room. "I don't know how much good this would do in a court of law," she said, snapping on a pair of gloves, before going to the dog. "Hi boy. You've had quite a day."

The dog relaxed under the sure and careful hands of the vet. She ran cotton swabs over the his neck by the collar, bagged them and the old collar, replacing it with another one. "Hold him while I swab his mouth."

"What's this?" She put the swab she'd been using into a bag and got a pair of tweezers. "There's something wedged between his teeth."

With Jessie's help holding the pup, she deftly extracted a bit of blue material.

"I bet that's from what the killer was wearing." Jessie turned the bag over in his hands as he studied the remnant. He had a bad feeling.

With a small bandage on his leg, and refreshed with food and water, Sam was ready to go as soon as Jessie finished a series of phone calls.

Rather than heading toward the dog pound, Jessie turned the van toward the Sheriff's office. He knew Petree was already there. That was one thing he had learned while on the phone.

After parking, Jessie checked his phone and tucked it into his shirt pocket. "Ready to go in Sam?" Helping the pup out, Jessie patted Sam's head. "Let's see how you like

Sheriff Petree now, buddy. And how he likes you."

Jessie opened the door and walked through the lobby where State Troopers stood, drawn by report of a murder in a small town that had few local resources. Nodding, he made his way to the sheriff's office, knocked, then entered at Petree's yelled, "Come in!"

Petree looked up from papers that covered his desktop. He scowled. "What are you doing here? Why is that mutt with you?"

Hackles arose on Sam's back as a growl came from his throat. The wolf-like eyes stared at the sheriff as if he were prey.

Petree pushed back from his desk, putting more distance between him and the dog. As he did so his torn sleeve slipped back to reveal a bloody bandage.

"You killed that man," Jessie said, eyeing the bandage.

"You're crazy."

"Crazy like a fox. Or rather like a dog—say like Sam here." Jessie allowed the pup to lunge closer to Petree. Growls grew even louder.

"You'll never guess what the vet found in his mouth." He waved a plastic bag containing the blue cloth.

Petree's eyes widened, then he sneered. "Sure I killed that scum. But that little bit of cloth doesn't mean a thing. This is my town. And you're nobody."

"Yeah, but those State Troopers outside heard you confess." Jessie held up his phone. "You can come in now."

"Damn dog," Petree muttered as a trooper cuffed him.

LOIS CURRAN

Born in Arkansas, Lois Curran spent most of her childhood in Salem, Oregon before her family moved to Lebanon, Missouri when she was fifteen. She now considers the Ozarks her home.

An avid reader, writing has always been a passion. Lois decided to become a full-time writer after she retired from her position as Director of Nursing at her local health department. As a Registered Nurse, she uses real world details to create believable characters.

Cruising and traveling are high on Curran's list of favorite things to do. She also enjoys taking pictures of her family and friends and sharing them on social media.

Curran is a member of Ozark Romance Authors, Sleuths' Ink Mystery Writers, and American Christian Fiction Writers.

PAYBACK

J im knew that when the wind blew, Paula's windows in the old house she'd inherited from her grandmother came alive with the overwhelming, rhythmic thumping sounds that frightened her: Swish, swoosh, whiff, whoosh, whizz. Peeking through the window, he watched Paula put both hands over her ears. Why did storms upset her? She thought she could control everything and everybody, a step above everyone around her. But he knew how she reacted to storms, and he'd waited until just the right one brewed to make his move.

The backdoor lock in the old house was easy to jimmy open, and he found himself just inside her tidy kitchen. He trekked to the old-fashioned swinging door that separated the kitchen from the living room. The dark kitchen made the perfect place for him to watch her in the lit next room.

Paula must have heard something because he saw her glance over her shoulder and he was sure, well almost sure, she had a foreboding her life was in imminent danger. Fingers of anticipation crawled up his spine while she stared at the doorway and he willed her to enter the kitchen. He had a nice gift waiting for her. He smiled and drew the dagger from its shield. *Come on in. I'll have the last laugh this time.*

He waited. He knew her routine and it wouldn't be long before she came into the kitchen to grab a beer from the fridge. To calm her nerves. Yeah, she was for sure gonna need it tonight. He knew her routine because he'd sat through a similar storm with her. When it ended, he'd let down his defenses and had declared his love for her.

She laughed.

She slowly eased up from the sofa and ran her shaking hands down her pant legs. How could a storm affect someone so much?

When she pushed through the swinging door, surprise spread across her face and she said, "How did you get in here?"

He walked toward her and chuckled when he saw naked fear light up her eyes.

"Get out of here."

He twirled the knife. "You aren't in charge anymore."

"Please don't hurt me."

"Aww, she begs." He ran his tongue over his lower lip and leaned over to gaze into her trembling eyes. "Oh yes. I am going to hurt you. Just like you hurt everyone that falls under your spell."

"How did I hurt you? I never meant to hurt you. I never meant to hurt anyone."

"You have no idea what you do to people. But I'm gonna teach you."

The ego-maniac was crying now. "Please let me go," she begged. "I won't tell anyone."

He ignored her. She was right, she wouldn't tell anyone because she would not leave this room alive. He'd made up his mind. Never had he imagined he'd be able to kill another human being. That is, until he got involved with her. He gave her, not only his heart, but his soul as well. And what did he get in return? She laughed at him. Said she'd never be interested in someone like him. She taught him that beauty and brains are weak because they are so fickle. Now it was his turn and he intended to show her.

"Paula, the best teacher, the greatest instructor to lead us to true wisdom, is pain."

"Oh, no. Please. No."

"Oh, but yes. Watching you suffer is the most faithful teacher, Paula. Your pain will lead to clarity, and clarity leads to truth. You will finally be able to see what scum you really are."

"I am so sorry I hurt you. If you give me a chance, I'll make it up to you." She was shaking. He loved seeing her beg for mercy. She could ask for it but never be able to give it.

He watched her stare at the knife he rotated only inches from her face.

"Jim, I always liked you. I didn't want to get involved with anyone. But you always meant a lot to me."

He leaned closer. "You are acting much better toward me now. I'm very proud of you."

She trembled slightly, and he could see the fear in her eyes. A whisper of terror rippled through her. "Please," she begged. But he just laughed.

He ran the tip of the razor-sharp knife down her left arm, opening an angry red wound. She screamed. When she saw the blood leaking out, she started to hyperventilate.

"I bet you're sorry you treated me like dirt under your feet now."

"I'll do anything to make it up to you. Please don't hurt me anymore."

"That's not how this works. You did the dirty deed. Now you're going to pay."

He took a deep breath and plunged the knife into her chest, just under her left breast, hoping his aim was spot on. He wanted to slice into her heart just as she'd sliced his.

She slid down the counter and he let the knife ride with her. When she hit the floor, he twisted his revenge weapon a complete turn before pulling it out. Satisfied with a job well done, he turned the faucet on and scrubbed her sticky blood from the dagger.

DUANE LAFLIN

Duane Laflin is an internationally awarded illusionist. After decades of performing experience on five continents, countless tours across the USA, and being on stage with long term theatrical contracts, he retired to Branson, Missouri, where he took up writing novels. The adventures his characters experience are realistic. The amazing things they do really could happen.

Writing as a man of faith, although gritty and authentic in terms of depicting human nature, evil and violence in this world, his stories are without profanity or gratuitous sex. Duane's wife, Mary, is his muse, counselor and critic in the writing process. His dog, Bosco, is at his feet when he writes and motivates him, at regular intervals, to get up and go out and for exercise.

Along with writing novels, which are a recent venture in his life, Duane has written many technical books for magicians and a number of volumes used by those in creative ministry.

APARTMENT 207

"Are you sure you should be here?" she asked.

She was the bartender; I was the clown. Actually, I was the man wearing the clown suit.

I answered, "Whether or not I should be here, I need to be here."

"I don't think so," she said.

She was a twenty-something young lady with pink spiked hair, a low-cut blouse, gaudy yoga pants, overdone makeup, and, in my opinion, too many tattoos and piercings.

I wanted to say, "Look at you. My clown suit isn't all that far removed from your style. Maybe you don't belong here either," but I didn't.

"Clowns don't sit at bars drinking hard liquor," she continued. "You're supposed to be an example to kids and stuff like that."

I told her my story.

I am a detective. My office is at the police station in Eugene, Oregon.

Years ago, I discovered the need to balance the stress of my job, and the negativity that often fills my days, with something light-hearted. My life wasn't fun, and I wasn't fun. This needed to change.

I cannot exactly explain the reason, but I decided, in my off-duty hours, to try being a clown. Later I learned this is properly called "clowning."

It turned out that being a clown isn't as easy as I thought. There really is an art to it and it costs more money than I expected. Those big clown shoes don't come cheap.

I learned how to perform at birthday parties to finance my new hobby. I do it on my days off. It is like wearing a disguise and it works out great.

The kids, and usually their parents too, rarely know I am a cop. This sets me free to be silly. Better yet, forty minutes of doing funny things, and making balloon animals, is great therapy. It lifts my spirit.

I tell myself, Why should I spend $120 an hour for a therapy session, in which someone else makes me feel better, when I can get paid $250 an hour to do the same thing for myself? I make other people happy too. It's a good deal.

Earlier that afternoon, I parked my clown car, a yellow Volkswagen Beetle, with a big red nose on the front and polka dots all over it, in the parking lot of an apartment complex near the university.

As I clomped up the sidewalk, it dawned on me that the building where I was to do the party was also the site of a recent unsolved homicide. A twenty-eight-year-old woman, single and attractive, had been shot dead and left in the center of her carpeted living room.

Everyone involved in the investigation, including myself, was mystified by the crime. There was no sign of a struggle or domestic difficulties. The woman had no connections with drugs or any type of underworld element. It appeared to be nothing more and nothing less, than a random, senseless event. The kind that often turns out to be most difficult to solve, because logic doesn't apply. It is hard to make sense out of something that doesn't make sense in the first place.

No clues were left behind, not even a shell casing. Forensics later learned the bullet which passed through her heart had been fired from a 38-caliber revolver. Revolvers do not throw shell casings. That's all we knew.

I took the elevator to the second floor. A homemade poster taped on the wall above the elevator's buttons advertised the party where I would make my appearance. I knew, considering the proximity of the university, that the building likely housed many young families belonging to those temporarily in town to get a formal education. Every four-year-old in the building would probably be at the party.

The elevator door opened on a hallway with which I was familiar. The young lady who lost her life, Patty Saldano, had lived in Apartment 207. It was four doors down on my right. The birthday party would take place in apartment 215, at the end of the hall.

I was passing Patty's former apartment when I heard a voice behind me.

"Hey clown, what are you doing here?"

I turned around and saw a boy; I guessed ten years in age, staring up at me with a scowl.

In my squeaky clown voice, one I thought to be quite entertaining, I replied, "I am here for a birthday party. Doesn't that sound like fun?"

"It doesn't," he said.

Obviously, I thought, they did not invite him to the party.

Before I could think of something clever to say, something that might make him smile, he said, "Get out of here. I don't like clowns!"

I understood. It is the hazard of being a clown. A hazard I did not sufficiently comprehend until I became one. According to my personal, non-scientific survey, 50% of the people in this world are okay with clowns, 25% really love them, and the other 25% are afraid of clowns and maybe even hate them. The ten-year-old, to whom I was speaking, clearly belonged in the last category.

"Have a good day," I squeaked, and made my way down the hall to the birthday party, leaving him behind. I assumed he was giving me an evil stare, but did not turn around to look.

As usual, my entrance was met with smiles and giggles. A two-year-old cried when he saw me, but I am used to that kind of thing. My arrival delighted everyone else. I did my shtick, and it warmed my heart to see the kids, and their parents, having a good time. It wasn't long before even the two-year-old seemed glad I was there.

At the end of my forty-five minute performance, the birthday girl's mother gave me my check and I made my exit, leaving the partiers behind to consume cake and ice cream while watching the opening of presents.

Back in the hall, I found it once again unoccupied by anyone other than myself.

I made my way along it, again passing room 207. As I neared the door to room 205, I noticed it was open. A boy stepped out of it. The same boy I had seen earlier. He had heard me coming and was holding a pistol. He aimed it at me. It was a 38-caliber revolver, not a toy.

"I told you to get out of here," he said.

For a moment, I was speechless.

"If you don't leave right now, I will shoot."

Without thinking, still using my clown voice, I asked, "Where did you get that gun?"

"It is my dad's. He keeps it in the dresser by his bed. He doesn't think I know it is there."

An awful thought entered my mind.

"Have you shot the gun before?" I asked.

"Yes, I have."

I don't know why I did it. Maybe it was because, when in my clown suit, with a red nose pasted over my real nose and a curly yellow wig on my head, it is hard to be out of character. Whatever the motivation, I challenged him.

"I'll bet you haven't," I said. "I'll bet you don't even know how to make it work."

A dark look came into his eyes.

"That's what the lady next door thought, too."

Acid welled up in my stomach. I couldn't believe what I was hearing, but it matched my assumption.

I responded, yet squeaking like a clown.

"I have no idea what you are talking about!"

"Yeh," said the kid. "You don't. No one does. My mom was upstairs having coffee with a friend. I was home by myself."

"You were?"

"Yeh, I was. Patty had her door open, so I walked in and told her she should take her clothes off."

"You what?" I replied, still squeaking like a clown.

"She is pretty. I wanted to see what she looked like with her clothes off. She told me she wouldn't do it. Guess what I did?"

I waited for him to tell me.

"I went back to our place and got my dad's gun. Then I went back to her apartment. The door was still open. I walked in and told her to take her clothes off or I would shoot."

I started to cry, not like someone who is upset or hysterical, instead like someone who is terribly sad, because I was. The tears must have done something weird to my makeup. I don't know what it looks like seeing a clown cry, but that's what the kid was seeing.

He smirked. "Look at you. You are afraid. She was too."

With the squeak in my clown voice gone but still speaking at a higher pitch than normal, I asked, "What did you do?"

"She didn't think I would shoot her and told me I should go home. She said I had a dirty mind and, when my mom got back, she would tell on me."

"Did you shoot her?"

"Yes. Then I told her, the next time I asked her to take her clothes off for me, she had better do it."

Wow, I thought. This kid is messed up.

"Now that you know about it, I need to shoot you, too."

I watched him put both thumbs on the hammer, preparing to pull it back, and realized, this kid knows how to use the weapon. He was going to shoot me. There was no doubt about it.

Before he could fully cock the weapon, I kicked upward with my size 24 black shoe. It flapped forward like a supersized beaver tail and caught the gun under the barrel, flipping it into the kid's face. Seeing the heavy metal barrel hit him in the forehead, I was grateful the weapon didn't go off.

Although I was moving fast, everything seemed to happen in slow motion. As he fell backwards, I saw a stunned look on his face. I threw myself on top of him, pushing the gun out of his hands and pinning him to the floor.

A mom from the party, leaving early with two children in tow, stepped out the door as this happened and saw me make my move on the kid. She didn't see the gun.

"Help!" she shouted. "The clown is attacking a child!"

More people came into the hall. Since I stayed where I was, they kept their distance, yelling at me, telling me to leave the child alone.

Somebody dialed 911. I kept a hold on the kid, and made sure no one touched the gun, until my brothers-in-blue arrived. After I told them what the boy told me, they checked the revolver. In the chamber were five loaded rounds and one spent shell. Since I hadn't touched it, the only finger prints on the weapon would be his and his dad's. It was definitely the murder weapon.

The bartender, thinking I was at my story's end, which I

was, spoke.

"So, the kid really killed the woman?"

"Yes, he did."

"But why didn't someone figure it out earlier? Didn't anyone talk to him and his parents?"

I remembered the situation well. When interviewing the family, his parents, fiercely protective, had spoken for him.

"He was in our apartment the whole time," they said. "He couldn't possibly know anything about the killing, nor do we. And don't you scar his young mind with details about it. He doesn't need to know what happened."

Although I hadn't liked their attitude, I had pretty much agreed with them. Who wants to talk to a kid about a murder?

I told her, "They said there was no way he could know anything about it. It made sense, so we believed them."

"What is the world coming to?" she said.

I asked her for another drink.

"Sure," she said. "I understand."

DREW THORN

Andy Tarbox is an accomplished writer with a remarkable career spanning four decades. With a diverse background in managing and producing marketing and technical papers for prominent corporations and government agencies, Andy has honed his skills as a versatile wordsmith.

Under his captivating pen name, Drew Thorn, he has ventured into the world of fiction. His debut novel, "The Pinnacle Club," is now available on Amazon, captivating readers with its compelling storyline. Book two in the series, The Oligarch, is also available, while book three The Vineyard is being written.

Growing up on a dairy farm in upstate New York, just a stone's throw away from Vermont, Andy feels fortunate to have been shaped by the hard work and playful experiences of rural life. Attending Tamarac High School, a close-knit community where everyone knew each other, fostered lasting relationships that continue to this day. Following his high school years, Andy pursued his education at Cornell University, where he proudly graduated after joining the esteemed Alpha Gamma Rho fraternity.

Throughout his professional journey, Andy's life has been marked by transformative experiences. Starting in the farm equipment industry, he later transitioned to the nascent personal computer industry during the early 1980s. Seeking new horizons, he delved into the world of smart cards, becoming an expert, and managing the migration from magnetic stripe to smart card technology as an executive at MasterCard.

Fortunate to have traveled extensively, Andy has had the opportunity to explore six continents and has accumulated over a million miles on United Airlines. His work has taken him to numerous cities worldwide, including vibrant metropolises such as Manhattan, Chicago, Palo Alto, and Sydney, Australia. While he has traversed 49 out of the 50 states, Alaska remains a destination that he aspires to visit, still on his bucket list.

Beyond his passion for writing, Drew finds solace in various activities. He enjoys gardening, cows, and the artistry of woodworking. While travel used to hold a special place in his heart, he now appreciates the comforts of home, acknowledging the challenges that come with the modern travel experience.

Proud of his loving family, Andy draws strength from their achievements. His wife, Judy, is an esteemed college English professor, while his son, John, excels as a commercial truck driver. Daughter Lizzy serves as a Captain in the Army, currently stationed in Jordan, and continues to make remarkable contributions to her field.

Embracing yet another transition in his life, Andy finds immense joy in the freedom of writing novels, where the only limits are the boundaries of one's imagination. Residing with his family in the serene Ozarks of Missouri, he relishes the tranquility of Midwestern life, providing the perfect backdrop for his creative endeavors.

For more information about Andy Tarbox and his captivating works, please visit his official website at https://www.drewthorn.com.

SEEKING REVENGE

Baytown, Texas

K ent had imagined exacting vengeance against DinoGas for the last five years. Tonight, would be an enormous step forward.

As he sat with his partner and lover, Kendra, at the picnic table overlooking the Baytown, Texas refinery, months of planning were finally going to turn into action. "Let's review what we know. This is the perfect spot to hit DinoGas. We know this is one of the largest refineries in the US, and much of what they make here is highly flammable ethane, heavier than air, the liquid ethane will flow across the ground as it explodes.

Kendra smiled and looked into his eyes, "Yes, this will let us get back at DinoGas for killing your parents. It is hard to imagine how they suffered, burned alive after the DinoGas tractor-trailer full of gasoline t-boned them."

"The ten-million-dollar settlement was a rounding error to the DinoGas bottom line. After a third to my lawyer and a third to the government, it added up to less than five million. The real concern is this refinery is an environmental disaster. DinoGas needs to be stopped."

Kendra said, "Are you ready? Everything is in the

backpack, and you practiced getting over the fence and know where to go."

Kent gazed into her eyes, "Absolutely. I'm amazed there's no concertina wire. The drone has been spectacular in helping us map out the perfect locations."

Kendra drove from the picnic area to the dark corner of the massive three-thousand-acre facility while Kent rode shotgun. She slowed and pulled over on the shoulder, gave him a big kiss, and Kent was off like a shot. Easily up and over the fence.

He jogged the half-mile to the first cracker. Behind the huge, insulated storage tank, he installed his first charge onto the ethane line, wrapping it tightly with gray duct tape. Set off a firecracker in an open hand. You will get burned, but if you make a fist. Boom, your hand is gone.

Kent worked his way around the plant, dressed as an employee. The night shift ignored him. Finally, all four charges were planted in critical locations. Kent spotted an unused golf cart and drove back near the drop spot.

Kendra picked him up. "How did it go?"

"Smooth, not even a question."

Back at the picnic table, Kendra poured two Lagavulin Single Malt Scotches on the rocks from the cooler in the backseat. At the same time, Kent prepared a cheese and cracker plate. They had a full view of the plant half a mile away.

Kent sipped his scotch and looked at Kendra. "Ready for fireworks?"

"Oh yeah, let's rock DinoGas's world."

Kent hit the first number on the speed dial list. A massive explosion went off, and it rocked them hard.

Kendra's eyes were like saucers, "WOW, that was amazing!"

"They deserve it! I can't believe people can live here with the poisonous stench from the factory."

"Look at those flames shooting over 300 feet into the

sky."

"Well, another fifteen minutes, we set off the next one."

Every fifteen minutes, they set off another bomb, a total of four.

Kent reflected, "You know the FBI will try to find us."

"Of course, they will try, using the location from this now dead cellphone, but our hotel is an hour away on the beach."

Parked a few blocks from the hotel, Kent removed his worn dirty DinoGas baseball cap and changed out of his DinoGas uniform. Next, he pulled off his fake mustache, beard, and wig. In the dark corner of the parking lot, Kent swapped the stolen plates for the correct ones for the rental car.

Kent looked up at the stars. "Mom, Dad, I hope you know we got revenge, and the sweet thing was it was DinoGas's money from the settlement that paid for all this, and it is only the beginning."

The next morning both the local and national news was dominated by the explosions at the refinery. All the experts pointed out that due to the location of the blasts, it had to be an act of terrorism. Others felt it was the work of a disgruntled employee.

Kent and Kendra had a leisurely breakfast at a nearby diner and listened to the waves gently breaking on the shore. Driving about four hours north and west, Kent dropped Kendra off at the Austin Airport long-term parking lot, and then he returned the car. To be safe, they were taking different flights to return home to Seattle, Washington.

Kendra flew home on Alaska Air, and Kent flew back on Delta. Once together again at SeaTac airport, they grabbed an Uber to their favorite upscale restaurant specializing in fresh Pacific seafood.

Over dinner, Kent said, "I think we need to do a lot more to protect the environment. What do you think of inviting Mark and Ellie to come out for a week and brainstorm ideas?"

Kendra looked at the ceiling and then back to Kent. "I think that is a brilliant idea."

Two weeks later, Mark and Ellie joined Kent and Kendra at a luxury home on the ocean outside Florence, Oregon. It had a huge open floor plan and views of the ocean and a large deck.

Walking into the large open foyer, Mark and Ellie were stunned by the all-glass two-story windows facing the ocean.

Kent said, "Welcome to our retreat for the next week."

Ellie was wide-eyed. "This is amazing. Perfect."

After a scrumptious steak dinner and dessert, everyone turned in with plans for serious discussions in the morning.

Kendra slipped into bed. "It was so wonderful catching up with those guys. It's been months and nice to see they are doing so well."

Kent rolled on his side facing Kendra. "I agree, I can't wait till tomorrow to see what the four of us can do to save the environment."

After a long slow cuddle, they were sound asleep to the sound of waves breaking on the nearby shore.

With the Pacific Ocean feet away from their perch on the deck, all were bundled up against the brisk morning air. The smell of the ocean fills their lungs with a refreshing and salty tang. The rhythmic sound of crashing waves provided a soothing backdrop to their conversation, as they huddled closer together, seeking warmth and camaraderie.

Mark started the discussion. "I have given this a lot of

thought. What I am about to suggest will be dramatic."

Kent leaned forward. "I agree it will take something massive to turn this ship around. What are you suggesting?"

"I have a way that we can kill the electric power grid for at least decades."

Kendra nodded. "Ok that would be huge. How would you do it?"

Mark leaned back in his chair. "The power grids around the world are controlled by supervisory control and data acquisition systems, SCADAs. These are large, powerful, and highly secure computer systems. We can't attack them directly and win. But the networks have thousands of programmable logic controllers, PLCs. These are really simple, and they monitor things like voltage, amperage, and temperature and report back to the SCADA. The vast networks of SCADAs are interconnected and collectively control the grid."

Kent said, "Sounds complicated."

Mark replied, "Oh it is, and it's not. We simply use the network to change a small amount of code in the PLCs so that at a specific time they all lie. We cause a surge in one part of the grid, and it cascades like lightning across the entire system. This will blow up huge transformers in sub-stations all over the country. In this plan, across the world. Lights out."

Kendra looked perplexed. "Won't they just replace transformers?"

Mark smiled. "They can't. The big transformers are purposely built for a specific sub-station. It takes at least a year to build one. There will be tens of thousands that will need to be replaced. Plus, they will not have electricity to build the components, let alone the whole transformers."

Kent said, "The plan is brilliant. I'm in. Let's work up our high-level strategy."

Mark in a serious tone said, "Please understand,

millions, perhaps billions of people will die within a month."

Kent had a wry smile, "We will get our environment back and can rebuild the world. It will be worth the cost."

Look for the novel "The Environmentalist" by Drew Thorn in 2025 to find out what happens.

JEN KENNING

Jen Kenning was born in Iowa and has called Southwest Missouri home for "the important part of her entire life." She always loved hearing and reading stories growing up. Her love of stories slowly morphed into a desire to spin her own tales. Jen has been a maid, waitress, cook, horseback riding trail guide, insurance adjuster, fire and theft investigator, customer service technician, and a reference librarian, among other things. Her favorite jobs were trail guide and librarian. She currently lives on a family farm with her son and too many pets and is working on her first full-length book.

COSMIC JUSTICE

*H*ow can I feel cold enough to shiver? It's 80
degrees tonight.

"Miss Stonehorse, I need you to come with me
down to the station. You will need to give a formal
statement."

*Maybe it's all this blood. Enough blood to soak my shirt
and with the breeze blowing through the window, yes, that
must be why I'm cold. I wonder if any of this blood is mine.
I wonder if that bastard is dead. I hope Darla is going to be
okay.*

"Miss Stonehorse! Miss, can you hear me? Sanders! I
thought you said the paramedics checked her out. She's
awake but unresponsive. I think she hit her head or
something."

"They did look her over and said she has no apparent
injuries, the blood belongs to him. She is probably in
shock. Captain said that if she isn't talking in the next few
minutes, we will transport her to the hospital for a psych
eval and hold her there until we get a statement," Sanders
said.

*I think they are talking about me. That psych hold thing
doesn't sound good. But a hospital will clean me up. That
wouldn't suck.*

"Sanders, do we know who the guy is yet?" asked the other cop.

"No name yet, but the female victim came to on her way to the ambulance and told the E.M.T. that the guy was trying to rape her," Sanders replied.

"So, we don't know who, but we know what this guy was. A garden variety dirtbag rapist. You ask me, this little gal did the world a favor putting that one down. I just wish she'd snap out of it and talk to me," said the other cop.

"No one asked you, Jenks. You get most of your exercise jumping to conclusions. Let's complete our investigation before you throw a parade for the cute little killer girl," Sanders said.

Cute little killer girl? Is he talking about me? Oh Goddess, that means that the guy is dead. I should probably feel worse about that, I thought just before I passed out.

I woke up to the sounds of a ruckus. Unsure of how much time had passed, I looked around and found that I was on a gurney outside of the dorm building. The source of the ruckus was Michael, my Michael. He was arguing with the police detectives. *What the hell is going on, what happened?* Then it all came flooding back to my memory. I screamed for Michael as I struggled against the loose straps keeping me on the gurney. An E.M.T tried to stop me as she finished tightening the straps, and I shoved her away. Finally free of the gurney, I launched myself at Michael as he bounded over to me, having shoved past the detectives. They were sputtering mad.

Michael scooped me up, big ugly tears, bloody clothes and all. Later he would tell me that through the sobbing I was trying to tell him what happened and kept saying that "he is dead, that bastard is dead."

"Hush my love, I've got you, you are safe," Michael assured me. He began walking away towards his car, still carrying me. The detectives just about went into orbit.

"Hold on there, who are you? Where do you think you

are taking her?" the one called Sanders demanded of Michael, who, to his credit, kept right on walking.

Sanders started to pull his service weapon, but Jenks laid a hand on his arm to stop him. I could see this happening over Michael's shoulder. Michael paused and said, "Do not pull that gun on me unless you want it given back to you in pieces. You will be hearing very soon my details."

I had nearly stopped crying, and the sound of Michael's voice, with its rich Israeli accent, further soothed me.

"Hey buddy, I asked you to stop. We need her to answer some questions. Don't make me arrest you for obstruction," Sanders said, following along in Michael's wake.

Michael stopped and wheeled around to face the oncoming detectives.

"I am taking Miss Stonehorse to a quiet place where she can eat, sleep, and get cleaned up, then tomorrow I will escort her down to your precinct to answer your questions and make a formal statement. This will happen after she has awakened of her own volition and had proper food. You will not detain us."

Just as Sanders was about to argue, Detective Jenks said, "Sanders, the chief just radioed instructions to let this guy—" he pointed at Michael and me by extension— "go and her too. Chief said tomorrow will be soon enough for her statement."

It was clear by the look on his face that Sanders did not like being overruled. Michael turned to walk away, but I squeezed his shoulder and whispered, "Hang on a minute."

"Is Darla all right?" I asked.

"I guess you'll find out tomorrow if you show up for your statement," Sanders snarled.

"Jeez Sanders, stop being an ass hat," Jenks said, and he continued, "Yeah, the other little gal is alive, on her way to the hospital and seems like she will be okay. Get some rest, you had a helluva night little lady." Jenks nodded his head at me with something like a smile.

Michael took me to his apartment, a spacious but spartan loft above a flea market. Not a word was spoken until after he had sent me to the shower, clothed me in cozy sweats and settled me on the couch. "Fen, it would be good if you told me everything now. We will make sure your version is cleaned to minimize any blowback," Michael said, as he put a steaming cup of coffee in my hands.

I accepted the cup and took a drink of the camel-colored goodness. He knew how I liked my coffee, strong enough to peel paint with a bit of cream and no sugar. "My version is that I fought for my life and won, barely. "What 'blowback'?" I asked tersely.

"That man, I saw his face. That was him and if the authorities find out there is history, it could become complicated," Michael said.

I sucked in a deep breath and blew it out. I knew I would have to tell this story to Michael and subsequently several times to the police and probably a bevy of random lawyers.

"I was just getting home; I had been at the campus library. I unlocked the door and went inside. I noticed the small table by the door was knocked over and I called out to my roommate. 'Darla are you home?' I heard a muffled noise, like a shrill grunt, then there was a thud. I ran across the living room and down the short hall. The door to Darla's room was open and the lights were off, but I saw the shadow of a man on top of Darla's bed."

"How could you see a shadow if the lights were off and how did you know it was a man?" Michael asked.

"There was a bit of light coming in through the third-floor window from the streetlights. I guess I didn't know it was a man at that time, just a figure, hell it could have been Darla," I answered as the scene played out in my head.

"What happened next?" Michael prompted.

"I flipped on the light and said something to Darla. I don't remember what I said because the moment the light came on everything went crazy. I saw Darla on the bed, there was blood on her head. I saw a man, yes in the couple seconds in between I was sure it was a man, kneeling on top of Darla. He was wearing a mask; the kind people use in cold weather. He yelled and came at me, we fought."

"More details, Fen. The police will dissect your statement. The man was not wearing a mask when I saw him," Michael said.

"Fine." I shut my eyes to better see the scene in my mind's eye. "He yelled 'you!' and he lunged off the bed and grabbed my shoulders with both hands. I used my elbow to break his hold on one side and struck him in the neck on my follow through just like in class. Then I smashed his face with my knee and shoved him as hard as I could. He fell down and I wanted to run away like you taught me, but I couldn't leave Darla, she wasn't moving, but I had to believe she was alive." I swiped the tears running down my face. *When did they start?*

"It's okay, Fen, you did great. What happened next?" Michael said.

I looked up at Michael and noticed a softness in his eyes that was not evident in his voice. Ever the professional, my teacher, my friend, my knight, my lover. Tonight, he is my inquisitor.

Nodding in resignation to the task at hand, I took a drink of coffee, which had become unpleasantly cool.

"The man got up, he pulled a knife from somewhere, it just appeared. He came at me again. I turned to avoid the knife and I grabbed his wrist. I punched him in the throat with my other hand. There was a struggle. I was kicking and hitting him. I cannot tell you the order of the blows, it was too fast. All I could think was 'control the knife', the knife was pointing down and coming at me again. I grabbed his arm with both hands and turned into his body, bringing the knife around. His thigh was right there, I sunk it to the hilt in his leg." I looked at Michael, hoping for a sign that we were done with this interrogation. We were not.

"At what point did his mask come off?" Michael asked.

"What difference does that make?" I countered.

"The man that tried to rape you eighteen months ago is dead. At what point did you know it was him? Make no mistake, I am proud of you and believe that cosmic justice has been served but, in today's society someone will try to make you the villain because someone died at your hand."

"His mask came off after he fell out the window. He was holding onto the window ledge, and I reached for him, I wasn't going to let him fall. His mask was partly off, I guess it had caught on something. I pulled it loose and saw his face. His eyes were so cold and full of hate. He said, 'You bitch, where is your boyfriend now?' 'Clearly I can save myself this time,' I said, and I crushed his fingers with a strike of my elbow. He let go of the edge and fell."

"Good, now you tell me again. We will practice tonight, so the statement you give to the police tomorrow will be airtight," Michael said.

After going over the incident at length with Michael and about six hours of sleep, we drove to the police station. Michael held my hand as we walked towards the steps leading to the main doors of the precinct.

I stopped and turned to Michael. "Michael, thank you. I'm alive because you taught me how to fight."

"I taught you Krav Maga, you are alive because you did not give up. The moves don't matter without the will to use them."

I nodded in acceptance and said, "Right then, let's get this over with."

SAGE HUNTER

Sage Hunter is a multi-talented artist, writer, and educator who has dedicated her life to pursuing creative passions and spreading the love of God through her work. With a solid foundation in graphic design from Ozarks Technical Community College, Sage honed her artistic skills and spent 15 years as a graphic artist.

Driven by a thirst for knowledge and a desire to inspire others, Sage embarked on an academic journey, earning a Bachelor of Science in Writing from Drury University and a Master of Art in Teaching and English from Missouri State University. She then spent eleven years teaching English and then art.

Recently retired from teaching, Sage has embraced her calling as a full-time writer and artist. As a Christian, Sage strives to exemplify God's love for her family, friends, and all those she encounters. She believes that to live is Christ and uses every opportunity to make a positive impact in the world.

For more information about Sage and to explore her inspiring portfolio, visit her website at http://www.sagehunter.org

SAVANNA STORM

Dark thunderclouds loomed over the vast African Savannah, casting ominous shadows on the land below. The air was thick with the scent of death and decay, and even the natives were fearful. For ten weeks, mangled animal corpses had been turning up all over the region, ten killings in total. Despite that, no one had any clue who or what was behind the carnage.

Maureen Jones, a journalist for National Geographic Magazine, was working in the area with Professor Raymond Ball, a disheveled geologist. One day, Maureen left the compound to photograph a newly discovered set of ruins, hoping to capture some stunning images for her article. She figured since an animal was killed the previous night, it should be relatively safe to venture out on her own.

As she dug in the earth, searching for shards of pottery, she stumbled upon an unbroken jar. Curiosity piqued, she peered inside and found a rolled-up piece of leather. She carefully examined the item and replaced it in the container for the professor to see. But as she turned to leave, a sudden gust of wind caught her off guard, and she lost her bearings. When she looked up, she found herself surrounded by a thick wall of dust; the wind howling around her.

Maureen pushed forward, the storm growing fiercer with each passing minute. She soon realized that she was lost, and panic set in. As she tried to retrace her steps, a shadowy figure emerged from the haze, grabbing her from behind. She struggled to break free, but it was no use. The figure dragged her off into the storm, leaving behind only her pack and a few scattered items.

Professor Ball worried when Maureen did not return by dusk. He sent out a search party, headed by Mike Sparkle, to look for her. When Mike returned two hours later with her pack, it was clear that something terrible had happened. There were signs of a scuffle, but no blood or real footprints to follow. The sand was so loose, and the storm that came up wiped out anything they could use to track her.

"This is hers," the professor said, examining the pack. He pulled out the clay jar and the leather document inside. "This looks like a map. I'll have to inspect it. Maybe it will give us a clue what happened to Maureen." He thought, why would someone stop this? Professor Ball suspected the clay jar with the map pointed to something someone didn't want to find. What could it be? Sacred burial grounds? A lost treasure? Professor Ball thought we needed to find Maureen and why she had disappeared.

Morning came, and Mike Sparkle checked in with the professor before heading out. "Mike, I'm wondering if Maureen's capture has anything to do with our investigation."

"Could be. Nothing else is happening except the regular anti-poaching crews, and that's nothing different from what they've been doing for years."

Professor Ball pulled out the map. "Are you familiar with this area?" He pointed to the area on the map marked with some unknown symbols. It's a small canyon a few kilometers from here. "Could there be caves there?"

"It's possible."

"Let's take a party out and look for Maureen."

"Do you think someone is protecting something out there from our discovery?" asked Mike.

"I don't know. Little is known about the history of this region, which is why we are investigating. We're trying to find out anything we can about the past civilizations of this region."

"Ah, if we find an advanced civilization in this area, it would undermine the thought that the people of Africa, other than the Egyptians, were incapable of advancement. It's a type of racism practiced by much of the world to keep the population under control."

"That's ridiculous. We must find Maureen safe," said Professor Ball. "Mike, can you get a search party together at first light? I don't want people going out by themselves. There's too much danger with animals being mangled and now Maureen missing."

The following morning, as the storm finally subsided, Mike Sparkle and the Professor set out to find Maureen. They checked out crevices and corners, looking for any sign of her. Suddenly, Mike let out a short, bird-like whistle. He had found some tracks. Carefully, they inched into the rocky outcrop and peaked around the corner in a cave-like area.

They saw Maureen. She was tied up, but there was no one else around. Mike tried to get Maureen's attention.

She looked desperate. "Help!" Her voice was muffled by a bandana tied to cover her mouth. Mike looked around furtively for her captor but saw no one. He ran over to Maureen and untied her.

"They left hours ago," she croaked. Her throat was dry. "They didn't want us looking here. I think they were hoping I would die in the dust. Whoever is doing this may use animal deaths to keep people away. I heard them talking. They speak English, but they have an accent. There's some evidence of an advanced civilization." The professor's eyes widened.

"I've heard some natives say no one believes the people of Africa are capable of an advanced civilization, and they want to keep it that way," remarked Mike.

"Why?" asked Maureen.

"It's just like any other society. Power and money rule. They are protecting their power at all costs," said Professor Ball. "You would think in a country where the majority is black, this wouldn't be the case, but just as everywhere else, it's all about controlling the narrative. Those in power don't want to lose it.

Maureen's face was pale. "We have to get out of here. We need to find what they're hiding and expose it to the world."

The trio hurried back to the compound, the sense of danger growing with each step they took, but they were one step closer to their proof.

Mike, Professor Ball, and Maureen reported their findings to the authorities, who launched an investigation into the matter. The search party that found Maureen became the catalyst for a larger movement toward uncovering the truth about the ancient civilization hidden in the savannah. After months of diligent work, the archeologists found what they were looking for: evidence of a highly advanced civilization that existed centuries before anyone had previously thought possible. The discovery challenged long-held beliefs about African history and sparked a renewed interest in uncovering the continent's past.

As for Maureen, she came out of the ordeal stronger and more determined than ever. She wrote a book detailing her experiences, which became a bestseller and helped to raise awareness of the injustice faced by many indigenous peoples. She returned to the savannah to continue her work, inspired by the hope that there was much more yet to be discovered.

The storm that initially threatened to derail the team's work became a metaphor for their resilience and determination. They had weathered the storm and emerged victorious, their spirits unbroken, and their wills stronger than ever. The legacy of the savannah storm would live on, a symbol of what could be achieved through courage and perseverance.

HAIR TRIGGER

The width of a human hair is exactly .08 centimeters. If that is any indication of how sensitive the hair trigger on the Beretta sitting on the table was, she didn't know that she wanted to touch it. But it was her or them. She took the clip and slapped it into the grip of the gun. As it clicked into place, the quality of the gun was obvious. It felt heavy in her hands, but she knew she would have to use it effectively if she would survive.

She took the stairs to the cellar and waited. If they didn't come down, she wouldn't have to shoot. She found the darkest corner and moved some boxes of clay pots in front of her, and waited. She had to calm her breathing; even a breath could give her position away. She didn't want to have to shoot anyone.

Her heart was pounding in her ears. She took deep, slow breaths. *Calm, calm.* She could hear them moving from room to room. It is only a matter of time till they come down here. She moved farther back into the corner. She pulled the boxes in closer around her. I need to make myself so small that they won't think I could be here.

The sound of their footsteps grew louder as they approached her hiding spot. She could hear them muttering to each other in low voices, trying to figure out where she could be. She clutched the gun tighter, her finger hovering over the hair trigger.

Suddenly, one box shifted, making a slight scraping noise. She froze, holding her breath. The men stopped in their tracks and turned towards her corner.

She could feel the sweat trickling down her back as she prepared to make her move. She knew she had to act quickly and decisively if she was going to survive.

Footsteps. She heard their brogans clunking over the floor. "You might as well come out from wherever you are. We'll find you."

As the men approached, she stepped out of the shadows. The gun held steady in her hands. The men froze, their eyes widening in surprise.

"Stay back," she warned, her voice shaking slightly. "I don't want to hurt anyone."

She was lost; he saw her cringing in the corner, desperately clasping a bottle of disinfectant; spraying him ferociously.

"In here, Dan. She's in the broom closet again."

"How did she get out of the room? I thought we had her door locked."

"I don't know, but we need to figure it out. What if she had gotten hold of something more dangerous than 409 spray to shoot with?"

"Come on, Darla, we'll take you back to your room. Dan, get her medication."

ROSALIE LOMBARDO

First and foremost, she is a storyteller…

Rosalie Lombardo is an award-winning author. Her articles have been published in national and international periodicals and online magazines. Her stories have appeared in Anthologies: *The Story Teller Magazine International, Traveling in the Sixties, Creative Collections* (Springfield Writers Guild), *Sleuths' Ink Mystery Writers 2019 and Spiritual Awakenings*. She was a featured columnist for a regional magazine.

Her love for diversity compels her to write in various genres. Her passion for children's stories inspired her to write a picture book for adults.

Rosalie has taught classes in metaphysics, meditation,

energy medicine, health and healing techniques in Chicago: Wright College, Harold Washington College, Resurrection Medical Center, Healing Earth Resources Training Center and throughout the United States.

She is a member of the International Society of Children's Book Writers and Illustrators, Springfield Writers Guild, Sleuths' Ink Mystery Writers and Springfield Writers Workshop.

Tappity Tap Tap, Nuggets of Gold a picture book for adults is available on Amazon, B&N, and other online retailers.

THE SPECTER

KABOOM! SMASH! — An explosion deafens us as something crashes through the kitchen ceiling.

We all jump at the bomb-like blast, but when we look up, there is nothing visibly there: no hole, no dangling pieces of broken ceiling, no busted pieces of wood, no floating plasterboard dust; nothing except the smooth, freshly painted, stark white plaster staring down at us.

Gram screams, "Yaoooow, what is this?" One moment she is frying fish, the next she grabs the kitchen towel from her shoulder and feverishly slaps the floor around her legs as if thrashing a vicious dog. Frantically she slaps her legs and stomps her feet, trying to shake off something from a source no one can see.

My brother, sister, Mom and Dad are sitting at the kitchen table, and I am standing two feet away from Gram.

"What's the matter?" I yelled.

"Get away, get off of me, STOP, IT'S BURNING!" She is talking like she's been set on fire from the bottom up.

We are witnessing an inexplicable phenomenon. I don't believe in ghosts or superstitious nonsense, yet Gram is living a nightmare where she is the target.

Mom trembles, and blurts, "I'm scared." She tries to

stand, but her knees buckle and she falls back onto the chair.

Dad shoves me away from Gram and positions himself behind her in case she collapses. I see nothing around her but sheer agony on her face. I know Mom thinks it's a devil; that's why she buckled. My younger sister is frozen. I scream at Gram, "There's nothing there!"

"Yes, there is!" she screams back. "FIRE, FIRE, I'm on fire!"

We are witnessing her terror and it's as real as if she is being barbequed alive.

Mom's sensitive stomach feels the urge to defecate, and she makes a mad dash to the bathroom.

"Something's there I tell you!" Gram shouts, "My legs are burning up!" Her sixth sense kicks in as she realizes this is a psychic attack and asks, "Who sent this demon?"

I'm trying to make logical sense of Gram's sudden excruciating pain. Maybe the veins in her legs ruptured. That might explain the burning sensation, but it doesn't explain the horrific blast we heard crashing through the ceiling.

I know there are energies in this world that science cannot explain. I also know the power of two trumps the power of one. I kneel next to Gram, and my hands begin to mimic hers. We are both beating her legs. I am helping ward off this evil energy as we command into the air, "Go! Get out of here! Go back from where you came!"

Mom returns as Gram grabs a fistful of salt from the large pink glass container sitting on the stove and throws it on her legs. She grabs another fistful with one hand and the container with the other and scatters salt around herself. She throws salt in the four corners of the kitchen, scatters fistfuls on the floor around the table, and then out the back door.

The demeanor on her face calms and moments later she says, "It's gone."

My brother blares, "What the hell was that?"

Gram knowingly sighs,

"Chico."

Mom chokes at the thought of Gram's insinuation, then stammers in disbelief,

"What are you saying?"

"Chico threw that bomb at me," Gram said. "I wasn't expecting it."

Chico is her brother-in-law, my great-uncle. There was bad blood between them. In 1948 he accused her of poisoning my grandfather, his brother. I was not yet born, but I know firsthand as I have seen the hate letter he wrote to her. His accusation was sent via airmail from Malibu, California, just three days after her husband died. The letter firmly established his deep-rooted treacherous, unscrupulous and toxic nature.

Gram and Grandpa Ross were geographically separated for twenty-eight years. After Grandpa Ross immigrated to Chicago from Sicily, Gram was left behind due to immigration law changes which severely restricted the flow of new immigrants from Italy.

It was almost three decades before Gram was granted permission to immigrate to the United States. Eight months after her arrival, Grandpa Ross' sudden death devastated her. Their furniture was repossessed. She did not know the language. She was left penniless and jobless with no place to stay. My Grandpa's five-hundred-dollar insurance policy, originally naming her as beneficiary, had her name crossed off in red X's and Chico's name inserted in bold black carbon print. The emotions from the stolen insurance policy couldn't compare to the rage she felt when Chico's letter arrived with his accusation. She kept that letter as a caution to always watch her back. She knew what he was physically capable of - evidenced by his banishment from the City of Chicago by the superintendent of police. She also knew he dabbled in black-magic but didn't realize until now, the extent of his knowledge.

"Mark the time," she said. "He lost this round."

It is 7:00 p.m., Saturday, November 19, 1977; I have experienced my first paranormal phenomenon.

Five hours later, the telephone's ring sounds off like a fire alarm waking everyone up. The phone in this house doesn't ring at midnight unless there is something drastically wrong. Dad picks up the phone. His look assured me someone died.

It is my Great Aunt, Giuseppa. She wants to speak to Gram.

"Maria, please forgive him." Giuseppa pleads. "I know he wasn't a good person, but he is still my brother."

In a tone harder than concrete Gram responds, "God forgives, I don't."

Chico is dead.

Gram slowly shakes her head up and down in silence, admitting her insight was on target.

"He tried to take me with him," she said, "but he lost the battle."

We may never know how that deafening sound blasted through the ceiling or how Chico was able to throw an invisible firebomb from over 2,000 miles away. And, even though death makes us physically nonexistent, the large pink salt jar on the stove is always full.

JJ RENEK

JJ Renek's debut novel *Payoff* will be released in Fall of 2023. Now retired from a career in medicine, she's turned to writing fiction. To date, she has penned seven medical suspense novels, all coming soon, and numerous short stories across various genres. JJ makes her home with her husband in the 'Show-Me' state where she writes full-time.

THE GOOD NEIGHBOR

Thick this case bugged her. The whole thing – the location, the evidence, the neighbor – all of it had occupied her time for most of four weeks, and Detective Enid Walsh felt frustrated they were no closer to solving this than when they found the body. Well, when they were summoned to a scene with a body.

The call from the decedent's dear friend and next-door neighbor struck her as decidedly strange. The woman informed them she had just discovered her closest friend, Buffy Flowers, lying face down in her Peach Tree condo. And what a shame, she'd said, Buffy had mussed her hair and drooled on her expensive white carpet. Can you imagine?

Upon their arrival, the whole setting seemed weird... too orderly, for one thing. And the dear friend, Karoline – with a K – Hamilton, had fussed over making them tea, poo-pooing their questions with a wave of her hand and an offer of fresh lemon cake. Enid and her colleague, Detective Duane Thomas, had obliged the woman's gracious offer, thinking she would eventually settle down and talk with them. But now, Enid had grown weary of the woman's daily calls asking questions and offering 'helpful tips' regarding the investigation.

Enid stared at the photographs and the list of items they had found lying about on Buffy's antique mahogany dining table. She turned to the plastic packages and again examined what they had retrieved.

A half-eaten cookie... bearing a coral lipstick imprint.

A teacup – *Royal Doulton* China, Karoline had informed them – tipped over, a dried teabag stuck inside: *Twining's of London*, Lady Grey black tea.

An expensive writing pen positioned near the teacup, cap screwed on tight.

A stamped envelope, unaddressed, containing a ticket to the upcoming Atlanta Flower Show, found at the other end of the long table.

Now, who eats a cookie with only their lips, leaving an obvious lipstick imprint behind?

An edentulous person, perhaps, or someone trying to mislead? And, no neat nick allows a turned-over teacup, with a dried teabag stuck inside, to lie about. Unless, of course, that person took a sip without removing the tea bag, lurched, knocking over – but not breaking – the fragile cup in the process. And where was the liquid stain from the tea spill? Mopped up without a trace or a residual watermark? Doubtful. DNA testing was still pending, but interestingly, the teacup and pen were devoid of fingerprints.

A knock interrupted her musings. Detective Thomas stuck his head in and asked, "Have a minute?"

Enid arched a brow, his signal to enter.

He closed the door, and said, "I just got a call."

She pointed to a chair in front of her desk. "So, what kind of call?"

Duane dropped onto the chair. "Karoline – with a K – Hamilton said we should take a look at something she found."

"What did she find?"

"Said it would keep."

Enid rolled her eyes. "Oh, God, please." Glancing at the

packages, she straightened in her chair and suggested, "Then, we must pay Miss Karoline a call."

— ◆ —

Their first knock went unanswered. As they stood before her door, they caught a whiff of something delicious wafting from within the condo. No doubt Karoline had made preparations for their visit. They delivered a second knock with a bit more force.

"I don't think it wise of us to partake of whatever she's baked up," Enid advised. "We're both full, have just had lunch. Got it?"

Looking disappointed, Thomas nodded his agreement.

Presently, they heard humming, and the click of heels preceded Karoline as she approached and opened her door. "Why, how nice of you to come calling today. I was just laying out refreshments. Do come in." She swung the door wide, welcoming them inside.

Dressed to the nines, Karoline showed them to her elaborately decorated living room, and indicated they should take seats on her rose-tufted sofa. The scent of air freshener hung heavy, competing with the baked goods aroma. Both sat where she directed them, eyed the silver tea and coffee service, and the various sweets set before them.

"Now, Mrs. Hamilton…" Enid began.

"Oh, please, it's Karoline…. but of course, that's with a 'K'."

"Of course. Now, Karoline, you called and told Detective Thomas you found something else related to Mrs. Flowers' death investigation?"

"Oh, dear, yes. You know, poor Buffy… she shouldn't have died so young."

Enid wasn't sure how Karoline defined 'young,' but eighty did not exactly fit her own definition of youth.

"So, Karoline, do you have the item you found?"

"Yes, it's here somewhere."

"Why don't you show it to us?"

"Good idea. I'll fetch it." Karoline rose and tottered off on her brocade four-inch heels – bangle bracelets jangling – toward a bedroom, or perhaps an office, in search of whatever she had called about.

Duane and Enid exchanged glances. Just as he reached for a shortbread cookie, Enid detected movement to her right. She turned slightly and watched a huge, white Persian feline creep languidly by an adjacent chocolate brown velvet armchair, his own bright green eyes fixed on them. Recovering from the distraction, and with only moments to spare, Enid seized Thomas' hand midair, relieving him of the cookie just before it grazed his lips. "Remember, no eating anything in this place," she hissed.

"Oh, right." With care, he replaced the pastry in its exact spot on the tray and brushed crumbs from his fingers.

"And, keep an eye on that feline," Enid added. The monster Persian, still staring, had assumed a seat on the velvet chair, likely his customary spot.

Karoline returned, clutching a small, black velvet bag. She perched on a blue wingchair, adjacent to the fireplace, and smiled.

Enid spoke first. "Is that what you found?"

"Well, it's in the bag." She paused, then dramatically opened the small pouch, and pulled out what looked like a lipstick case encrusted with jewels.

Enid asked, "May I see that?"

"Of course, but do take care."

Enid made a show, in return, of donning a pair of gloves from her pocket and asked, "And just where did you find that, Karoline?"

"Oh, at poor Buffy's."

Now, when had she been to Buffy's since her friend's death? Perhaps she had not relinquished all the keys a good neighbor might possess? Enid extended her gloved hand, and received the remarkable bejeweled lipstick from Karoline. Opening it, she wound the lipstick upward – bright coral. It appeared well-used. Studying the woman, she sniffed, noting no odor.

Karoline gushed, "Oh, dear, it was her favorite shade. She used it constantly." Smiling, she added, "I gave her that one a month ago... for her birthday."

Enid eyed Karoline and said, "We'll have to take it for testing, you know."

Karoline smoothed her slim skirt and managed an, "Oh, dear..."

Enid wound down the lipstick and secured the encrusted top. Displaying it in her hand, she asked, "Karoline, is there something else?"

Looking pensive, Karoline answered, "Oh, my, yes. I'm so worried about the ticket."

"Ticket?"

"To the flower show, the one you took." She frowned. "I so wanted to go with her, but she said, 'No, this is for someone else.'"

"Karoline, you – "

Wistful then, Karoline added, "What a shame she behaved so badly and had to go. It's just such a shame, isn't it?"

189

PASSAGE

They had asked for my help. To rid them or, more correctly, their place of her. I recall holding the receiver, staring at my bookshelf, not knowing what exactly I could do or how to approach such a request. The rather one-sided conversation ended with, 'Won't you please agree to come over later this week and discuss this?' Her obvious distress touched me. I'm afraid I consented, against my better judgement, to meet with them – just once, I said – and hear their entreaty.

I locked my car and stood at the curb, shoring up courage, and resolved to limit my involvement in such a drama.

The sun, low in the sky, cast long shadows across the well-groomed front lawn, the massive front terrace, and adjacent gardens. I remembered its appearance only a few years before when it sat vacant, sad and despondent, waiting for new owners, a tangle of overgrown vegetation clinging to its blackened stone walls. The amazing transformation had restored the gothic structure to its original beauty, a testament to their perseverance and love of history. Perhaps, also, to their considerable purse. But had they researched the place before buying? I would have thought so, which might have allowed them to approach their current problem without involving me.

Pressing the doorbell, I waited. Deep melodious tones rang out. Momentarily, I detected footsteps approaching. The door swung open, revealing a forty-something woman who wore not a look of distress, but a smile. The smell of freshly baked goods wafted through the open door.

"Yes, hello. Please come in." She opened the massive walnut door further to allow easy entry. I stepped through and stopped in the spacious, ornately-trimmed foyer. The scent of lemon oil hung in the air. "May I take your jacket?" she inquired.

I obliged, glad to remove it in the warm interior.

Reminder introductions made – we'd met at a party not two months before – she invited me into a cavernous room to the left of the foyer where her husband, who appeared less enthused than her, waited. An impressive cookie assortment and coffee service rested on a narrow table near a huge bay window.

"My husband Graham," she said, and gesturing toward me, "Darling, this is Ms. Antwerp, Anora Antwerp." He stepped forward and offered his hand.

"Anora it is. Pleased to make your acquaintance, Graham."

While helping ourselves to refreshments, he suggested, "Do sit down, make yourself comfortable."

Having settled, we enjoyed the first few bites of our selected pastries and sipped the steaming coffee, enduring a somewhat awkward silence.

I began. "First, I wish to compliment you on the restoration you've accomplished. The house is quite extraordinary."

They both thanked me, and Graham added, "The endeavor was well worth it." She agreed with a nod.

The room fell quiet again.

"Quite delicious," I remarked, around a bite of iced shortbread, scattering wayward crumbs here and there in the process.

She thanked me and, apparently fortified, dove in. "I know my call seemed strange, and I do apologize. We have a situation here... which has thrown us. I recalled our meeting at the Windsor's not long ago, and your comments concerning visitations. After discussing it, we felt we must seek your advice."

Eyeing them over the rim of the fine china cup, I asked, "So, what exactly *is* your situation?"

They paused, exchanged glances, and Graham answered. "Actually, we're not quite sure. It seems, though, that we have a restless spirit residing in the house. A spirit who may be trying to communicate with us. It's quite unsettling at times, though I believe we've gotten over our initial shock and fear."

"You live here alone?" I asked.

"Yes." He added, "We've no children."

"Had you investigated the history of the house before you purchased?"

"No, not other than the basics, structural integrity, all that sort of thing."

"And when did you first notice something off?"

"Shortly after we moved in."

She further explained, "At first it was only an occasional sound, a door closing or a rustling in an adjacent room. We dismissed them as the sounds of an old house, or our own auditory perceptive errors." She looked at Graham. "Then about four months ago, we found books lying open in the library, none of which we'd pulled or left out. Old books, a remainder with the house." She took a deep breath and added, "One night, soon after that, I sensed a presence hovering over me, awoke from what I thought was a dream, and saw a shadow – an image – drifting away from our bed and into the hall. Naturally, I was terrified. I roused Graham, but, of course, there was nothing."

"Has that happened since?"

"Yes, one other time."

"Quite unsettling, I must say," Graham added.

I regarded them, impressed with their relative calm, considering such remarkable experiences. Redirecting, I asked, "What sorts of books do you find left out or open?"

"Books of area history, old novels – mysteries, gothic horror – and various Greek tragedies."

"What a fascinating assortment. But, how may I help?"

"Being the town librarian, and familiar with the community's past, we thought you might shed light on what happened here, and assist us to find someone who might rid us of the presence."

"I see. So, why don't you show me the books which make regular appearances."

They abandoned their refreshments – forcing me to do the same – got to their feet, and led me into the paneled library. Immense bookshelves lined three walls, with tall paned windows claiming the fourth. What a fantastic chamber it was!

Refocusing then, I examined the six volumes they had pulled – all of which as they had described. I turned to them, and could not ignore their anxious, expectant gazes. How would I explain my conclusion?

After pausing, I said, "I believe you've met Gertrude Giddings, a woman who died some forty years ago, in 1980. Widow of the local doctor, she lived out all of her ninety years in this house, intending to pass it on to her surviving children. But, reportedly, they had no interest in the place and only wished to sell it to the highest bidder. It eventually went to auction and none of them ever returned – most are now deceased." I paused to reflect, then added, "I believe there may be one aged straggler left somewhere. At any rate, up to this point, none of their descendants have shown up, either."

A troubled expression briefly clouded her face. She asked, "How many children did Gertrude and the doctor have?"

"Five, but reportedly, only four survived. One died a young child, not unusual at the time. Apparently, though, her death seemed suspicious – some swore it a murder – but was passed off in 1919 to the Influenza. Perhaps Gertrude is attempting to provide clues, or solve the mystery herself."

"How intriguing," she observed.

"Quite so. Perhaps if you give her passage, she'll settle and depart in peace."

"And just how do we accomplish that?" asked Graham.

"I would suggest engaging the priest from St. Paul's, perhaps also the Historic Forensics professor at the College, and... yourself."

She couldn't conceal her surprise at my statement and stood staring. "What on earth do you mean... me?"

"Yes, you are key, Mrs. Grace Newland." I offered her a warm smile, and said, "Welcome home, Grace Giddings Newland, welcome home. Your great-grandmother is, no doubt, exceptionally pleased."

LARISSA TOWERS

Larissa Towers has been writing since she was a child. Her interests include romance, science fiction, and mystery. She lives in Arkansas and travels the world looking for new adventures. She speaks at writer's conferences and helps mentor independently published authors. She enjoys murders and mayhem, if only on paper.

THE WEDDING PICTURE

C ara grabbed the phone. "Sis, it's 6:30 on Saturday morning. This better be good."

"I think I have the stomach flu," her twin Mara replied.

"So?"

"I am shooting a wedding tonight at Belle Meade Mansion. Please do this one thing for me and I will never ask anything again. I promise."

"I'm not a photographer, I am an unemployed actress. Besides it's haunted. Some dude found his wife on their wedding night with her throat slit. He cursed the place and vowed to haunt it until he found her again."

"That was over a hundred years ago, I figure he found her by now," she laughed. "This is a costume wedding and a very important client."

"Going back to sleep now," Cara growled into the phone.

"It pays $500. Please, you can use my new digital camera, just point, and click. Check it after every couple of shots to make sure you've got pictures you can use."

"Five hundred cash?"

Cara arrived early at the antebellum mansion with her sister's digital camera in hand. Once again Mara had talked her into something stupid.

As she entered the foyer a man stopped her. "Why aren't you dressed yet?"

Cara stammered something about pictures, but his sparkling green eyes mesmerized her.

He bowed and smiled. "Todd Meade owner of Belle Meade at your service."

"Great costume," she added, admiring the 19th century suit and tie he wore, finished off with a black silk top hat.

"You are not properly dressed Miss McGregor, follow me."

"How do you know my last name?"

"I know everyone at our wedding." He smiled.

Okay she would play along; this wedding was costing someone's dad a small fortune. Hiring period actors was probably part of the package. She followed him up the winding staircase to the second floor. "Go inside there," he pointed to a door, "your dress was delivered this afternoon."

Sure it was, she thought to herself as she smiled. Once inside the room she noticed the lovely white gown on the bed. She had trouble with the buttons on the bodice. Sheesh, even the shoes had buttons. Once dressed, she surveyed herself in the long mirror, astonished at how well it fit.

When she went downstairs Todd was nowhere to be found. She checked the camera and got ready for the main event. She had to admit the costumes were a nice touch.

During the ceremony she snapped pictures of the couple. She stopped a few times and toggled back to check her work. In each shot she noticed a dark blurry figure standing behind the groom and looking at the bride. She hoped Mara could photoshop him out.

She continued to snap pictures relieved that the dark figure no longer appeared in the subsequent ones. Finally, it was time for her last shot of the night, the cake cutting. In the final shot, the blurry figure was back. When she looked closely at the picture, she nearly dropped the camera. The blurry figure wasn't blurry anymore and he wasn't looking at the bride this time, he was staring into the camera directly at her, and on his head was a familiar top hat.

Startled, she stumbled into a nearby gazebo. She placed the camera on a table nearby. To her surprise, Todd appeared beside her.

"You look flushed. May I offer you a refreshment?" He handed her a crystal cup and she sipped the tepid punch. He offered his hand, and Cara took it.

When Mara had not heard from her sister the next evening, she figured Cara was 'pissed' at her for making her do the photoshoot. The following day, she notified the police. All that was found was Cara's car, her camera in the gazebo, and her clothes on a bed upstairs. All the pictures on the digital camera were deleted.

The case went from a missing person to a cold case. It wasn't until two years later when Mara was shooting another wedding at Belle Meade, that she wandered into an upstairs bedroom looking for the bridesmaids. There on the mantel was a picture of a couple on their wedding day, along with several other pictures of the couple with their children and finally the couple in their senior years. When she looked more closely, the woman in all the pictures was her sister. She stared in horror as she read the placard beside the wedding photo.

Todd Meade, and his bride Cara McGregor, July 1885.

CURL UP AND DYE

It was just a matter of perception. Tracy saw himself alive, and I pictured him dead.

Wait, I am getting ahead of myself. I am an author, and when I wrote my series of mystery novels called *Curl Up and Dye,* I thought all publishers were trustworthy. The five completed novels centered around a small beauty salon in Arkansas and the amateur sleuths who worked there. Let me start at the beginning.

"Dogma-Swine Publishing. How can we help you?"

"Hi, my name is Larissa Towers, and I met your owners, Tracey and Mamie, at a writer's conference in Arkansas. They gave me their card and said to call when I got home." I took a deep breath and waited for a response.

"Yes, just a moment. I will get someone to help you."

I waited for what seemed like hours but was likely only a couple of minutes. A booming voice I recognized came on the line.

"Hey, welcome to Dogma-Swine, where we publish the extraordinary. Tracey Bowen speaking."

"Hi," I stammered. "I'm Larissa, and we met at a conference in Arkansas. I wrote the series Curl Up and Dye. You said to contact you when I got back home."

"Yes, I remember. I have spoken to the team about your books, and we want to offer you a five-book contract. We will publish one book every six months. Our in-house team of editors, publicists, and marketing gurus are excited about the series."

I couldn't breathe, I had been waiting tables at Friendly's for two years, and now my big break had happened. "Wow, thank you, Mr. Bowen. This is a great opportunity for me."

"We will email you the contract today, and once you sign it, you can send us your manuscripts. Remember, at Dogma-Swine, we support authors all the time."

I called my best friend Renda with the news. She was less enthusiastic than I thought she would be.

"Larissa, I have heard some things about this publisher. Did you talk to any of their authors? What are the terms of your contract? Hey, my sister-in-law's third cousin's hubby is a lawyer. Want me to find out if he will review the contract for you?"

"No, that's okay." I didn't have the heart to tell her that I was so excited when Mr. Bowen emailed the contract that I didn't bother to read it all the way through; I just read the part about royalties, e-signed it, and emailed it right back to him. I had attended workshops, and I knew the industry standard was 10-20% royalty, and they were offering me 40% net, so that was good enough for me. Plus, I had a call from their marketing team that afternoon to discuss promoting my book. It was only later that I learned there was no marketing team unless you counted their agoraphobic daughter, LeeAnn, who lived in Tracy and Mamie's basement with her pet rat, Dicky.

Six months passed, and no book, no answered phone calls or emails, and no contact with the publisher. They had a Facebook group called Dogma-Authors, but nothing new had been posted. I did get ahold of the company once, and the person on the other line said Covid 19 had slowed down everything, and they were running a few months behind. Covid 19? That was over two years ago? I found myself wishing I had read the contract more carefully.

Nine months later, the pancakes I was serving a customer clanged to the floor when the TV in Friendly's announced that a local publishing company signed a deal with Netflix for a new mystery series. The reporter sat across from Tracy and his wife, Mamie. Tell us about this new series you wrote, Mamie. "Well, it is called 'Curl Up and Dye,' and it is based on a group of amateur sleuths who work together in a beauty salon in Arkansas."

"Nooooooooo," I screamed, scaring the customers and prompting Mr. Lee, my boss, to send me home for the rest of the day to calm down. This time I did go to a lawyer. And 3600 dollars later, I found that you can't copyright a title, and if you change just enough of a story, it is no longer considered plagiarism.

Now I was broke, and my life's work had been stolen. But if it took everything I had, I would get them for ripping off my idea and manuscript. I filed suit immediately, and a letter arrived one week later.

Dear Author,

Due to circumstances beyond our control, Dogma-Swine is closing its doors. Covid-19 and the subsequent slowdown in publishing have resulted in a restriction on our profit. We appreciate your interest in publishing with us. We will return your rights to you per article 3.1.7. in your contract. In the future, we will form a new company, Curl Up and Dye Enterprises, and in a few years, we plan to continue our work in the publishing field. In the meantime, we are concentrating on Mamie's success with her soon-to-be-released series on Netflix 'Curl Up and Dye.'

Tracey & Mamie Bowen

I shredded the letter, but I would have my day in court, or so I thought. Three months later, another $5000 bill from the lawyer and I found out the suit had been thrown out for lack of evidence. Then I was fired from my job. That is when I decided I would get my revenge.

After I submitted my fingerprints and a notarized Arkansas State Police/FBI criminal background check form, I found a job as a pharmacy tech at my local CVS.

I waited for just the right time. Each day was as monotonous as the one before it. I had just about given up hope of ever getting even with those crooks, but finally, my patience paid off. Tracy came through the drive-thru late one day as the pharmacy was closing. Everyone was too busy closing out the daily receipts to notice me. My heart pounded when I told the drive-thru tech, "I think that prescription is in the back. I will get it for you."

Quickly I rushed to the back of the store and carefully removed the bottle I had prepared at home. It looked just like the real one. I couldn't help but smile when I handed it to the tech. Funny how easy it was to substitute strychnine pills for his weight-loss medicine. The two looked almost the same. It's amazing what can be purchased online if you know where to look.

My only regret? I wasn't there to see him...curl up and die!

DARCY GRACE

Darcy grew up as a Navy brat, following her father's career across three continents. This unique life experience has fed her imagination from a very young age. She was always conjuring up stories and filling them with unique, colorful characters, exotic locations, and one zany situation after another.

She holds a bachelor's degree with concentrated studies in education, psychology, and theatre arts. Her short stories have won multiple awards. She has a fantasy trilogy and a cozy mystery series in the works, with many more ideas bubbling around in her imagination just waiting to be released.

She lives in southwest Missouri with her son. Her goal is to be able leave her current nine-to-five job and transition into a full-time author and speaker role. She also hopes to find a final forever home close to the beach!

You can read more of her writing at AuthorDarcyGrace.com.

THE UNCONVENTIONAL EXORCIST

S am pulled up beside a black Lincoln town car in front of an ornate wrought-iron gate. He approached a tall thin man in an expensive suit who stood staring down the long driveway. Sam joined him and they both stared at the old Victorian-style house positioned on a large estate.

"Is this the Hawthorn Family Estate?"

"Yes, sir."

"I thought there was an auction today. Am I here on the wrong day? The wrong time?"

"No sir, it's the right day and you're right on time. I am Walter Herrington, the estate attorney handling the property sale."

"Nice to meet you. I'm Sam Wilson, potential buyer. So, where are the other people? I can't believe I'm the only one here to bid on this old house. I mean, it's obviously a fixer-upper, but it can't be that bad, can it?"

"Oh, the house is in pretty good shape. It mainly needs some TLC and cosmetic work."

"So why isn't anyone else here?

"Well, when Edna Hawthorn passed away, the estate was willed to her family. Several family members moved in then promptly moved back out, passing it on to the next one, and now none of them want it. They decided to sell the place, with the proceeds going to her heirs. It has been sold several times, but all the buyers back out at the last minute. This time it will go to the highest bidder. The family no longer cares about getting anything out of it; they just want it gone."

"Why?"

"Well… Um…"

"Yes?"

"You see… Well, it's like this…"

"Spit it out man!"

Walter took a deep breath. "It's haunted."

"That's ridiculous!"

"Yeah, well, um, whoever buys it gets the house, the contents and the surrounding seven acres of land. Are you interested in making a bid?"

"Shall we go take a look at it?"

"You are welcome to, but I am not setting foot beyond this gate," he said wide-eyed. "The key is under the front door mat."

"I will be back." Sam got into his car, drove up to the house and let himself in. It was a typical large Victorian with good-sized rooms and tall ceilings. A few odd pieces of finely crafted antiques were scattered throughout.

He was right, a bit of TLC and this place will be back to the grand estate of its hay day, Sam thought to himself. *Anyone would be a fool not to take it.*

"Any ghosts here?" he called out. The silence was his only response. "That's what I thought."

Sam drove back down the lane to the lawyer, sitting in his car. "I'd like to make an offer."

A look of shock came over the lawyer's face. "Really? You know once you sign the papers it is all yours. The family has made it clear that under no circumstances am I to take it back"

"I would expect nothing less."

"All right then. Fill in your offer here, sign here, and here, and it's yours to do with it as you wish."

As quickly as Sam signed, Walter grabbed the papers, gave Sam his bill of sale and jumped into his car. His tires squealed as he sped away.

With a shrug, Sam returned to his car and left to make preparations for his move.

◆

Two weeks later Harold watched from the attic window as Sam got out of his car followed by a chocolate lab. They quickly disappeared onto the porch. He heard the click of the lock and the slow creak of the front door.

"Here comes another one. When will these mortals learn that this is my house?" He turned and glided to a moose head hanging next to chalk tick marks on the wall. "Hmmm, this one makes 40, a nice round number, doncha think Morris? We are going to have fun with him and his little dog too!"

The moose head hung motionless in reply as Harold continued to speak. "So, Morris, what do you think we should try first... I agree... let's start tonight."

Back down downstairs. "Well Chip," Sam said, "what do you think?"

"Woof", came Chip's reply.

"You're right, let's unload the car, start dinner, check emails, pull out the sleeping bag and turn in. The movers will be here early tomorrow morning."

◆

CLANK! BANG! Moan.

Sam's eyes popped open. The room was dark. He looked around to see what woke him as another wave of moaning hit his ears. *Wind must be leaking into the house. Mental note, get supplies to fix that,* he told himself as he covered his head with a pillow and drifted back to sleep.

"He doesn't scare easily, does he Morris?" Harold commented to the moose head. "I like a challenge." Harold paced as he contemplated what to try next.

◆

The next morning Chip barked as the moving truck rumbled up the drive.

"Yes, Chip, our stuff is here." Sam opened the door to the movers.

Hello Sir, I'm Bill and this is Tom and we have your belongings."

"Nice to meet you. I have marked all the doors to coincide with the tags on the boxes and furniture. Don't hesitate to come get me if you have any questions," Sam instructed. "I've got to get back to work. Chip, you stay out of their way."

"Ruff," Chip promised. With that, Sam returned to the kitchen to continue working on his computer.

The movers started unloading the truck. Trip after trip back and forth all the while Chip followed their every move giving his sniff of approval as each item was placed in the house.

Harold watched the activity from the attic window. "Well Morris, we need to plan this just right. If we do, then we can get rid of all of them at once."

When the truck was about half empty. Bill and Tom sat on the front porch peering into their sack lunches. Harold knew his time had come. He left the attic, moving boxes from their nice neat stacks scattering them haphazardly all over the rooms. He flipped the furniture causing a complete mess of things before heading downstairs to repeat the process.

Back in the kitchen Sam didn't seem to notice anything,

but Chip was very aware of the strange happenings. He growled and barked at every box or piece of furniture that seemed to move on its own.

"Be quiet Chip. I'm working," scolded Sam.

It wasn't until Bill and Tom had finished their lunches and began to unload the last of the truck that they noticed boxes sliding around the room. Furniture was stacked this way and that. Nothing was where it had been placed. Then a toaster seemed to float across the room right between them and then smashed itself on the table with a loud CRASH!

Sam came running into the room. "What happened?"

Bill, wide-eyed pointed to all the chaos going on in the room as the couch finished upending itself.

"Why would you put a couch in the middle of the room, up on its side like that?" Sam questioned.

"Sir, I swear, we... we put it over against the wall."

Boxes continued to move across the floor as Chip followed them growling and barking. Tom seemed to be frozen in terror while Bill yelped as a box slid into him.

"I will have to get this floor levelled," Sam said and started to walk back into the kitchen.

"Wait sir," Bill stammered. "I...I think this place is ha, ha, haunted!" He swallowed hard.

"Nonsense!"

"Okay well, um... We only have a few more boxes. We'll leave them on the porch and go. Here's your receipt. No tip needed."

"That is fine by me." Sam shrugged and returned to his work as Bill grabbed Tom by the arm and pulled him out the door.

Back in the attic, this turn of events caused Harold to blow his stack. He started kicking and throwing things from one end of the attic to the other. He looked up at Morris and swore. "How can he be so blind? I'll get him yet!"

All the ruckus from the attic caused Chip to start

growling and barking at the ceiling. Sam looked up too. "I hear it as well, boy. I think we may have pests up there. What do you think, rats, raccoons, bats?"

Another growl was Chip's reply.

"You're right. It doesn't matter much. We'll get rid of those pests soon enough. Let's get some dinner."

"PESTS! He hasn't seen a pest yet!" Grabbing Morris' face, he looked straight into his eyes. "You know I can do this? Right? I will get rid of them yet!"

As the days went by, Harold continued to make a real 'pest' of himself. He would hurl items at Sam and Chip. Sam would just rationalize it away and Chip thought it was a game. He took great pride in catching the items and returning them to their rightful place.

Harold moved objects trying to trip them up. Both Sam and Chip had accepted it as normal and would just jump over the object as if the house was some kind of obstacle course. He would cause the lights to flicker and the cable and phones to crackle with static, but nothing seemed to phase either Sam or Chip.

Back in the attic, Harold was becoming more and more unhinged, shouting at Morris, trying to bang his head on the wall to no avail as his head kept passing through it instead. With a crazed laugh it hit him. "His dog is the key. I will get him through his dog," he explained to Morris.

The next day while Sam was on the phone with a client, Harold picked Chip up and floated him all around the room. Chip did not like this at all. He whimpered and tried to run away, but it was no use. His paws wouldn't touch the floor. He was helpless, running on air that would not let him go.

"Quiet Chip! I have a very important client on the phone."

Chip whimpered in reply.

Later that night Sam stepped out of the shower and wiped the fog off the mirror, completely missing the message warning him to "Leave or else."

This caused Harold to blow his top. "No more mister nice guy!" he roared.

Without warning, the sink and shower began spurting blood all over and more blood ran down the walls. A foul odor seemed to come from everywhere.

"Looks like we may need to have the septic system looked at. There seems to be a lot of red clay in the pipes causing it to back up," Sam said casually to Chip.

"I can't stand it anymore! I quit!" Harold screamed at Morris back in the attic.

That evening Sam sat on the couch, watching TV with Chip when a blast of cold air rushed through the room. The front door opened, then slammed shut. Sam smiled and pulled out a tiny key attached to a chain around his neck, opened the lock to a journal and placed another tick mark under the heading, 'Ghosts Evicted.'

"Well Chip, that took a week longer than I expected. But now that it's ghost free, let's get the place ready to sell. I have a lead on our next house."

Chip looked up at Sam wide-eyed.

THE NIGHT HE SAW RED

J eff arrived home from work promptly at 5:30 p.m. as usual. *Something isn't right.* He stood in the entryway trying to figure it out. *No squabbling teens, no scent of dinner, no dog running to greet him.* Then he saw it. A bright red envelope on the entryway table. Inside was a note on old-fashioned parchment in ink that looked a lot like blood.

We have your family! We are watching you!
Follow all instructions is what you must do!
No harm will come provided you do as we say
No cops, or extra stops is the only way.

His breathing accelerated; His hands shook. He continued to read.

If you want to see your family alive
Come to the corner of 5th and Westchester Drive.

Heart pounding, he grabbed his keys and raced for the car. Hands shaking, He could barely work the GPS. He squealed out of the driveway. Three long red lights and twenty minutes later, he pulled up to a vacant lot. *This can't be right, there's nothing here.* In his panic, he almost missed it—another unobtrusively placed red envelope taped to the signpost.

> Your family isn't far
> Make your way to Main Street and Smitty's Bar
> Go inside and ask for Joe,
> He'll direct you as to which way to go

Back in his car, Jeff's head spun. *What kind of guy could be part of this?* He gunned the gas, narrowly missing a parked car. A*n accident is not going to help my family.* He took slow deep breaths, trying to calm himself to no avail. "Curse this traffic!" he yelled.

Another long twenty-five minutes later, he pulled into the parking lot of Smitty's Bar. Slamming the car in park. Jeff sprinted for the door and burst through.

"Joe, who's Joe!"

A stocky guy behind the bar looked up. "That's me, be right with you."

"I don't have time! My family's in trouble!" shouted Jeff. *Maybe I've said too much. Maybe the kidnappers have someone here, watching!* Looking around, nerves on edge, a few patrons stared at him. He crossed to the bar in three strides, head down. "Look, do you have something for me?"

"Oh, you must be Jeff." The bartender spoke calmly.

"Yes!"

"I was told you would be by to pick this up." With that Joe retrieved a cell phone from beside the cash register."

"That's it? No red envelope? No Note?"

Joe replied with a shrug.

"Who told you I was going to come pick this up?"

"Some guy."

"Who was he? What did he look like?"

"I don't know, average height and build, brown hair."

"You're no help." Jeff took the phone and raced to his car. *Wait! This is my daughter's phone. Oh Lord, help me! Chloe is never without her phone.* He turned it on. A video popped on the screen. Hands shaking, he hit play. He watched his daughter recording one of her vlog posts. Then a muffled male voice in the background said, "Give me your phone, now!"

"No!" his daughter said in defiance.

What's she doing? Jeff thought. "Just give it to him," he pleaded out loud as if it would make a difference. Next, he heard her scream and the phone dropped camera side down. There were sounds of a struggle. Then that same muffled voice recited....

You know we are serious, as you can tell.
Continue to do as we say, and your family will be well
You will soon get what you are owed
Go to the fountain on the corner of High Street and Maple Road

The video ended. Pedal to the metal, he raced out of the parking lot. *All this time wasted back and forth across town. What's their endgame?* Jeff broke out in a cold sweat. When he reached the fountain, he double-parked and raced over to the water. There, sealed in a Ziplock bag, floating on the water, was another red envelope.

Another clue. Following clue after clue, across town and back again, he worried. *When'll this end? My poor family.* Nearly faint with apprehension, he spotted another envelope that read:

Enough time has passed.
You need to act fast.
Find the alley behind the Big Box store.
Follow the cloaked figure up the stairs and through the door.

Jeff jumped back into his car, his head full of fear and questions. *Who's doing this? Why my family? What do they want? Why the wild goose chase?*

Arriving at the alley, Jeff looked in all directions. No cloaked figure. *Now what!?* His eyes slowly adjusted to the darkness. Then a car pulled into the alley, blinding him with its headlights. He heard the engine die and saw a dark figure in a trench coat and fedora hat leave the car, ascend the staircase, and enter the door at the top.

Sliding out of his car, Jeff wiped the sweat from his brow. He shook as he slowly began to climb the steps with feet feeling as heavy as cement blocks. His breath came in shallow and quick gasps. Terrified, he placed his hand on the cool steel knob and slowly twisted. The door creaked open to darkness. What sparse light shown from the distant streetlamp did little to help his sight. Then he heard a low, deep muffled voice not too far in front of him.

"Step inside and close the door."

Jeff did as he was told. "Where's my family?"

Suddenly, the lights came on blinding Jeff's eyes. A roar of "SURPRISE!" flooded his ears. His eyes slowly adjusted, and he saw his family, friends and coworkers all standing around the room. Across the space spread a huge banner.

HAPPY BIRTHDAY!

It was written in the same blood-red text as all the clues he had been forced to follow. Jeff shook his head, fists clenched. "Do you all know what you put me through tonight?!"

"We had to keep you busy somehow," said Greg, his best friend since childhood.

So, it was Greg all along… Jeff fumed in exasperation.

Chloe spoke up. "So, Uncle Greg about that new phone

you promised me if I gave you my old phone."

Jeff cocked an eye, a sly smile slowly formed on his lips. "You know you can't buy one of them a new phone without getting all three of them a new phone."

The twins, Madison and Mason, chimed in. "We're getting new phones too! You're the best Uncle ever."

"What's that, a couple hundred a piece? I can handle that," Greg boasted.

Jeff pulled his daughter's phone out of his pocket and handed it to her. "Show him the phone you want."

"The one I really, really want?" she asked wide-eyed.

Her dad nodded with a sinister grin. Chloe tapped the phone of her dreams. Handing the phone to Greg, his eyes popped out of his head, "You can't be serious! I have to buy three of these!"

"Dead serious," Jeff said, slightly satisfied.

"I think I need a drink."

JANET KAY GALLAGHER

Janet Kay Gallagher is a Christian Author. My parents were readers, and my earliest memories are filled with fun trips to the library. My parents read the BIBLE and the CHILDREN'S CLASSIC STORIES to my brother Bob and me before bed. In the days before television, the newspaper and radio were our news and entertainment. Sunday morning, we ran out and got the newspaper and jumped in bed with Dad and Mom, and Dad read the comics to us. Like some of our favorites, TERRY AND THE PIRATES, DICK TRACY, LIL'ABNER, and DAGWOOD AND BLONDIE. Later in the day, he would read items from the newspaper about trees and planets and anything of interest.

Two librarians had a positive impact on my reading. Mrs. Warren made sure I was reading the books in my age group, she knew if I had checked them out to read. I was impressed by the personal care and guidance of Mrs. Warren.

I loved Mrs. Tierney's Seventh Grade Library Training Class. Checking out books and working in the school library was fun. Mrs. Tierney gave personal attention to the books I read and discussed them with me.

I enjoyed reading to my two boys Stephen and Ken. When Stephen was in fourth grade I was told he had Dyslexia. That explained my own reading problems. And why the librarians helping keep my reading up to my grade levels meant so much to me. When I was in school, it didn't have a name. Mom couldn't understand why I couldn't tell the difference in, The and the, since they were the same word.

I still read daily or listen to books read by my Kindle Fire. I'm also a big fan of Audiobooks.

Now I'm writing short stories and poems and my own books. I hope my readers will enjoy them and remember the stories.

WARM AND HAPPY

This story won 2nd place in the
Sleuths' Ink Mystery Writers
1st Quarter Contest 2023

I couldn't scream! I stood there, petrified against the wall, unable to move. It had happened so fast and unexpectedly. No warning.

I'd seen him kill the man on the ground a few feet in front of me. The knife flashed in the dim light of the alley. He bent and checked that the man was dead. Wiped his knife on his victim's shirt.

My heart pounded, I expected him to kill me. When he looked up, he saw me and frowned. He knew I saw his face and yet he turned and started to climb the alley steps to the next street level. He didn't even hurry.

I cried tears of release from years of abuse from the dead man. I went to him and picked up his wallet and keys from his pocket. Took the money and photos. Wiped my prints off with my skirt and left the wallet in a dumpster a couple of streets over.

Now I would learn to live. I went home and waited for the police to notify me of his death.

The first thing I did was turn up the thermostat to warm

my house. That was one of his control methods, ensuring I was always cold. I baked an apple pie while the pot roast cooked with potatoes and onions in the crock pot. I made a salad. Set the table for two as usual.

The death scene replayed in my head. How could the killer let me go? He knew I saw him. Did he know he saved me from a life of pain and abuse? Why am I still alive?

The man didn't take anything but his life. Why him? Did they know each other? The killer walked right up to him and didn't speak. He cut his prey and watched him bleed out. Wiped his knife and left.

It was several hours before the police arrived at my door. Detective Arnold Mays introduced himself and his partner, Shelia Bowman.

"Mrs. Lenord, is your husband Thomas Lenord?" detective Mays asked.

"Yes, what has happened?"

"He was mugged and killed in an alley this afternoon. His wallet was found empty in a dumpster a couple of blocks away. We had to run his fingerprints to identify him."

"Are you sure it's Tom?"

"Yes, ma'am."

"How awful," I said, and a few tears gathered in my eyes.

"If we can be of any help to you, here are our phone numbers. We're sorry to have to bring you this news. Goodbye."

When they were gone, I went to the kitchen and served myself some of the delicious dinner I'd prepared. I ate, and no one criticized me or the food or the house. No nasty fight or pain tonight. I stayed up most of the night and breathed easily. No yelling. No hurt feelings. No more broken bones ever.

Life alone would be good. I'd smile again and laugh out loud.

MURDER AT THE AUTOGRAPH SHOW

T om Everly set up his table exactly as he wanted it.
Perfectionist that he was made this mandatory. The
show had opened twenty minutes ago, and only a
handful of people, not connected with the event, had shown
up. He was sitting behind his table, drinking the hot coffee
one of the attendants had brought him.

He needed this show to bring in enough money to cover
him for the winter. His last movie was ten years ago. At the
height of his career, he was paid millions, and now it was
mostly gone. Tom felt demeaned, having to resort to
autograph shows for a living. It did pay well. He got a
hundred dollars for his signature on a photo.

Towns all over the country had annual festivals, and
celebrities came and were greeted like royalty by loyal
television and movie fans. Many of the fans didn't
remember their real name but called them by the character
they played years ago.

Tom met many of the same artists at the next festival. It
was a regular circuit they followed. Sometimes, they were
there for the autograph show, and other times, they were
the featured speakers for different events. Many of them
became friends and others only associates.

Tom had been in a movie about fifteen years ago with

Allen Donnelly, who had deliberately tripped him, and a horse stepped on his leg. He had pain from it most of the time. He was careful not to let himself limp. When he was tired it was harder to conceal it.

Allen had started attending the autograph show this year. Since they had been in a couple of movies together the organizers wanted to seat them together, thinking they could work off each other for more sales for each of them.

Tom had started asking about Allen when scheduling a show and refusing to be seated by him. Now here they were again, seated next to each other. Tom had spoken to the organizer and was told they couldn't change it this time. He had almost packed up and gone home but decided he needed to stay and make the money.

By 10:30, the traffic had picked up. Tom and Allen, and many of the celebrities, were selling their books, photos, autographs and other items of interest from the shows where the celebrity was featured.

Tom was always amazed that people asked him why he did what he did in a single episode, and that they remembered and could quote it word for word. Much of the time, he didn't remember the episode they were talking about. He became good at telling them something that fit their request and often added a behind-the-scenes story that pleased them. He wanted fans to feel like they got their money's worth when they talked to him or bought from him. Many of the people who came by his table didn't have the money to spend but wanted to tell him how much they liked his movies and TV work. He smiled and acted like he had just been waiting to meet them.

Today and tomorrow, the organizers of this Cherry Blossom Festival had assigned him a helper, Mary Chase. She was a grocery store clerk at the local market, taking in the money and giving change. Tom noted that she counted the money back to them. He hadn't seen that done recently except at these small-town events. A good money person was always a great asset. And today the money was flowing well.

A short time before noon one of the assistants for the festival came by and told them, "Lunch is ready in the room behind the stage."

Tom said, "Mary, go and eat lunch and when you get back, I'll go have mine."

He noticed that Allen had gone immediately, and his assistant Lucia Mays stayed at the table. There was a lull in the traffic and he and Lucia talked awhile. She told him about the town and other events occurring at the festival. She had a pie entered in the contest. The three winners would be announced at the dinner tonight and then the pies would be auctioned off to raise funds for the festival.

Tom watched Allen walk back to his table. He wondered if Allen had had a liquid lunch instead of whatever the festival provided. He was weaving a bit.

Tom heard Lucia ask, "Allen, are you feeling all right?"

Allen said, "I'm okay. Did you sell anything while I was gone?"

Lucia pointed out a couple across the room who had said they would come back when Allen was there. "They want a photo with you and will buy an autographed movie photo."

Not long after Allen got back, Mary came and sat down with Tom. Several celebrities were coming back to tables and others were leaving. The fans had thinned out for lunch.

Tom excused himself. He stopped at Allen's table and said, "Allen you look ill. Do we need to get you some medical help?"

Allen exploded. "You'd like that wouldn't you! Then you wouldn't have me as competition. I'm fine, leave me alone."

When Tom came back from lunch, he thought Allen looked worse. But he didn't say anything.

The sales were good, and fans were thick about 2:30

when Tom heard Lucia gasp and saw Allen slump over his table.

Tom went over and felt his pulse and found none. The police and paramedics arrived quickly.

Allen Donnelly was pronounced dead at the scene.

Sheriff John Roberts asked Tom, "What did you see since you were seated close to the victim?"

"I noticed he was weaving as he walked back from lunch and wondered if he was on drugs or had drunk his lunch instead of eating. As I was going to my lunch, I asked him if we needed to get him medical help, and he got mad at me. When I came back, he looked worse, but I didn't say anything since I had already made him angry. I heard Lucia, his helper, ask him a couple of times how he was feeling, and he snarled at her that he was all right.

"Later I saw him slump over the table, and I went over and felt for a pulse and didn't find one. The authorities were called. I was told the visiting people here were taken to a room, the people with booths were asked to stay in their places and the doors were locked."

The sheriff said, "I heard you didn't want to be seated by Allen Donnelly because of a long-standing feud."

Tom said, "He caused a painful accident years ago and I didn't want to be seated by him. But the organizers thought since we had different photos from the same movie that we would probably both sell more.

"Allen started on the Autograph Circuit this year. I have been doing it for several years and make a good living at it. I decided I could deal with sitting near him since it was to my advantage. His death doesn't hurt or help me in any way."

Sheriff John spoke to Mary Chase, Tom's helper. "Mary, someone I spoke to said you and Allen had a lively conversation in the lunchroom today. It looked like both of you were mad and arguing. Tell me what it was about."

"He was a jerk. When we were setting up for the show,

he was complaining about Lucia not being pretty enough to be his helper. And he made many other petty remarks about people in the room. All morning he made rude remarks about the people who came to these events, even ones who had purchased items from him. In the breakroom, he came to my table and said if I was prettier, he might have asked me out. I told him he should get over himself. He grabbed my arm and squeezed it hard. I went outside to my car and finished my sandwich. Then, when he slumped over dead, I felt he deserved it.

"When she was questioned, Lucia Mays said pretty much the same thing. How Allen acted nasty and contemptuous about the people who attended the festivals. I asked why he came to them if he hated everyone so much. He said, 'Silly girl, for the money of course.'"

Everyone was questioned and sent home. The festival concluded the next day. Since several people mentioned the victim looked bad after lunch, an autopsy was performed, and when the results came back, an overdose of a drug used for diabetics was found. Murder or suicide? It had a good amount of evidence of suicide by Allen's actions. Being offered medical help and refusing to acknowledge a problem. But Sheriff John felt in his bones that it was murder.

He had thoroughly investigated the sellers at the show and their helpers. He had attended school with most of the local helpers. Mary Chase was homecoming queen that year and he remembered she left for Hollywood shortly after graduation. A couple of years later she was back home and worked for many years at the grocery store as a cashier. She didn't talk about Hollywood. Had she met Allen Donnelly?

Sheriff John and Deputy Myers rang the doorbell and waited for Mary Chase to open the door. She invited them in and offered them tea. They refused and were seated at the table where she was having her tea.

The sheriff said, "Mary, I remember you went to Hollywood after graduation. Tell me about it, please. Did you meet Allen Donnelly there?"

She looked them each in the eye and started. "I was an extra in the western SAGEBRUSH, with Tom and Allen. One of the photos Tom was selling had me and the other saloon girls in the background with him playing poker with the outlaws. He didn't recognize me as I sat helping him all day.

"Allen, of course, remembered me and followed me to the breakroom. He made a few nasty remarks about our time in Hollywood. He ranted at me low enough others couldn't make out the words, and he gestured around as he put on a performance for the others in the room and didn't see me slip the pills into his drink. I knew for months he would be here, so I brought the pills. He had already made me a murderer, so his death benefited me. While working on that show we became lovers, and I thought that included marriage, so he arranged a marriage. We signed papers and everything. I was so happy when I came from the doctor's office to announce that we were pregnant. He denied that it was his baby and insisted I have an abortion. Everyone was doing it, and it was safe. Afterward, I went crazy with grief and guilt and was hospitalized for almost a year. I couldn't get over the fact that he had made me a murderer by killing our baby.

"After I left the hospital, I found out our marriage wasn't real. He had hired actors to set it up. That was the end for me, and I moved home. That is why I never married.

"When I heard Allen would be part of the autograph show, and I knew that he was a diabetic, I put my plan in action. I started taking a pill from my friends each time I visited with them. Since they were taken over time, they didn't realize I was taking them.

"I volunteered for the show and asked to help Tom

Everly. If he recognized me, he would be kind.

"I'm glad I killed him." As she slumped over, her teacup fell to the floor and broke.

A LAWYER'S NIGHTMARE

T he envelope was sitting on the desk when I arrived this morning. My paralegal Joan Thomas told me she put it there when it came in yesterday. It was from a lawyer friend Marshall Scott. I had my coffee and donut before opening it.

On top was a letter from Marshall telling me that my former client, Samuel Leonard had died and left me this short story. There was a second envelope with a few pages in it. The title was HOW TO…By Samuel Leonard.

I had to think back over several years to remember that case. It must be at least fifteen years ago that I defended him on a charge of murder. As soon as I heard his story, I knew I could get him acquitted. I was glad he was innocent, so it would be easy to go to trial with right on our side.

The first page was addressed to me.

Dear Mr. John Owens, Attorney at Law

I wanted you to know. I truly appreciated you defending me for the murder of Roland Acer. He had bullied me from first grade through high school. Then he got a job in sales at the same firm where I worked as an insurance adjuster. The bullying and bad jokes at my expense continued. This went on for about ten years. Roland got fired because he wasn't selling enough policies and had been harassing some of the female employees. There were also complaints from some of his customers. He moved on and drifted around for several years, doing whatever jobs he could get.

I knew my chance would come one day. So, I made up plots to get rid of him and get away with it. This went on for a long time. When the opportunity arrived, I was ready.

I studied you as well as my victim. I knew you were honest and sometimes got into problems because you wanted all your clients to be innocent.

Roland got a real estate license and was working for a good company. I made an appointment under another name to see a listing, and when he got out of his car, I shot him in the heart. I was back far enough not to get blood on me. Right away, you could tell he was dead, but I checked to make sure. I put the gun on the ground near the body and walked away.

It was about five hours later that the police knocked on my door. I invited them in and asked why they were there. Had something happened to my sister-in-law who was now a widow?

They asked to see my gun. I went to the locked cabinet and was shocked to find it missing. They informed me they had it, and that it had been used in the murder of Roland Acer. They took me to the station. I insisted I didn't know the gun was missing and that I hadn't seen Roland in years, which was true. After a long time, someone suggested I call an attorney. I came up with your name and you came to see me.

I explained that I had been in a busy restaurant, and that I spent a lot of time *dining* there, and then went home. Not much of an alibi, but you believed me and saw that no one with common sense would convict me on their flimsy evidence.

Mr. Owens, you were brilliant when you put me on the stand and showed the jury that even though this man had made life hard for me years before I could not possibly have murdered Mr. Roland Acer.

You said, "No one would wait that long just to get even for bad behavior. What kind of criminal would leave the gun next to the body with their prints on it? Someone else must have done it and set up the frame for my client. You must acquit this innocent man. Mr. Samuel Leonard has been framed!"

The jury freed me, and I got away with murder. But karma always evens the score, shortly afterward I was diagnosed with lung cancer. It took away the ability to walk and breathe well, and so the great life I was planning was gone forever.

I thought you should know that crime really doesn't pay after all.

Sincerely, Samuel Leonard

CALL THE POLICE!

"I thought I saw a light in the house across the street. Emily and Jon are gone until the 6th of the month. Phil, call the police. There it is again. A light is moving around in there," Annie said.

"Stay out of it. Jon already thinks you are a nosy neighbor. He sees you watching out that window all the time. If there is someone in the house, they can see you too."

"Did you agree with Jon? I don't think I am nosy, just concerned. Oh, look, that light again. Call the police. They might be robbing the house. Maybe doing drugs over there."

"Annie, you are impossible. I didn't see a light."

"Call the police, Phil. It is the proper thing to do. If someone broke into our house, wouldn't you want a neighbor to call the cops?"

"Well, if I could convince the robbers to take you with them, no." Phil chuckled.

"You are so good-looking, I guess you could easily find a replacement for me and all my problems. Maybe a woman who fancies bald men with a paunch." Annie put on her hurt face.

"Baby, you know I need you. Our vows said until

death."

"So, now you want me to hurry up and die?"

"You know better than that. Don't I take good care of you?" he implored.

"Yes." She hiccupped. She looked around at her lovely clean home. She glanced at her gnarled hand and leg which didn't move well. Her long illness sometimes made her forget how much Phil does for her.

"I am sorry for saying that. I am grateful to you for everything you do." Her eye caught the light across the street again.

"Phil, call the cops. There is a light flickering in the house," Annie said.

"Maybe you are seeing things. I haven't seen anything over there. If the police come and no one is there, they will think you are a crazy old lady. I don't think we should get involved," he said.

"If it's kids in the neighborhood they might come after us if we call the police. It could be dangerous. Let's stay out of it. Jon has insurance if they are thieves or vandals."

Annie glared at her husband of 34 years and pressed the button on her medical alert unit. "9 1 1, how can I help you?" the operator said.

"I think the house across the street from me is being robbed. I keep seeing a light that is moving around the house." Annie ignored Phil s up-thrown hands and shaking head.

"Are you at 19342 Pine Crest? Do you know the house number across the street?"

"Yes. It is 19345, Jon and Emily Nelson's house."

"What is your name?"

"Annie Gordon."

"We are dispatching a car. Thank you. Did you need anything else?"

"No, thank you," Annie said.

When the call ended, Phil said, "Why did you do that? I

told you not to get involved." He stormed into the kitchen. He had cooled down and brought their supper. Turkey sandwiches and a banana, fresh coffee, and a piece of coconut pie.

Just as Phil sat in his big blue chair, the police drove up across the street. They surrounded the Nelson's house and came out finally with three young men in their teens. Put them into one patrol car and that car drove away. An officer crossed the street and rang the doorbell. Phil answered.

"Hello, I'm Officer Jackson. Are you folks all right? "

"Yes," Phil said.

"Please step outside, sir," the officer said.

"Why?" Phil asked, stepping out the door.

"Have Mrs. Gordon step out also."

Phil said loudly. "Annie, come out here."

Annie got her cane and came to the door and stepped outside, too. "I called you," she said.

"This is just for your protection. Just making sure no one came over here and was holding you hostage. Thanks for calling us. Those boys were eating Pizza, and ice cream they found in the freezer, and cookies. They were watching TV. They said they knew the house was empty and just wanted a place to hang out for a while. Several houses have been used by them over the last few weeks."

"Because you called, the mystery has been solved. They never took anything except the food they ate, and they put the food containers in the peoples' inside trash. That's how the homeowners knew their house had been invaded.

The boys' parents will get them out and be surprised by this latest prank on their part. Thanks again," officer Jackson said.

Phil helped Annie back into the house to her light blue chair. "Well old girl, you solved a crime from your armchair. I will reheat our coffee to celebrate and we'll eat our supper."

ANGRY WOMAN'S REVENGE

Another dismal day, raining and gray. More time to dwell on that cheat who had taken her only valuable possession. The only thing left from her father's estate. The exquisite, matched set; emerald necklace, earrings, brooch, and bracelet, given to her great-great-grandmother for her act of kindness by a potentate over a century ago.

Terry loved that set and wanted it back. The police weren't getting anywhere in finding Arnold Akers or the woman he was thought to be with. They hadn't found the jewels in the regular places they looked for valuable stolen goods.

Detective Paul Leland had told her, "Since we know someone posed as you at the bank to open the deposit box, Arnold must have found the deposit key in its little envelope with the box number on it and took it from your purse and had someone pose as you.

"Are you sure he was the only one who had access to your house and purse? When was the last time you went to the deposit box? Did he ever go to the bank with you? Did he know about the emerald set and the money, or did he just get lucky?" he asked.

"I have friends that I meet with in groups usually. Most

of the time, I meet them somewhere else. My friends have seen me wear the jewelry, but I don't think Arnold knew about them. I never discussed my bank with him. Perhaps he saw an envelope from them in the mail on the table. I usually put the mail on the table until I go through it.

"Detective Leland I feel sure it had to be Arnold who took it. I haven't seen him since it went missing."

The detective said, "Mrs. James, I understand there is a very interesting story about how your relation came into possession of the set. Has it ever been written about?"

"Yes. A Great-aunt wrote a short story about the adventures of a woman who saved the ruler of the land she was visiting with her husband. She overheard a plot against him. No one thought that she might know their language. They spoke freely in front of her. She told the king, and the assassins were caught in the act. By being forewarned, he wasn't killed. He was grateful and awarded her the valuable jewels. Before deciding what to give her for the good deed, he asked what her favorite jewel was, and she told him Emerald. I have several copies of the book. If you want to read it, I will loan it to you. But since it is out of circulation, it must stay in the family. The book is: A WOMAN WHO SAVED A KING A True Story of Paralee Adams by Anna Merriweather."

She loaned him the book and he promised to keep in touch and try to locate Arnold.

She liked the idea that Paul Leland would keep in touch with her. She had been a widow for seven years and was lonely sometimes. That is how Arnold's flattery had interested her.

Terry listed everything she could remember about Arnold. Where he liked to go, bars, restaurants, malls, bookstores. Books and More Books, is where she met him. It was like a whirlwind romance. He was always there, never leaving her alone for any length of time. He was charming and had her fooled. She really thought he cared for her. When he started to talk about marriage, she told him she wasn't ready.

The next day was sunny. Terry drove to the car rental office and rented a car. She started her rounds of all the places she had listed, and on the third day, she saw Arnold at Wendy's. He had taken her there several times. He was with a lady about her age. She didn't fit the description of the woman who had opened Terry's bank deposit box. Terry found Arnold's car and attached the tracker she had purchased. When he and his new victim left, she was able to follow at a safe distance. She knew he always watched his rearview mirror. Terry noted the woman's address and continued to follow Arnold. When he parked in the driveway, she noted his address. Terry turned into the driveway with her blue rental car.

She called detective Paul Leland and told him. "I found Arnold. It looks like he has a new victim, a woman about my age. Her address is 17224 Mayfield Street. When he left her house he drove to 9736 Prairie Grove Lane and walked in without knocking or ringing the bell. I think he is living there."

"If he follows the pattern with me, he will be going to see her again tomorrow about 10 A.M. Sometimes he smelled of perfume, and I got the feeling that he had been out with a woman before coming to see me. Maybe he is seeing several women at a time."

"I want to follow him and see how many women he is stringing along. I know he watches his rearview mirror constantly, so I would be careful."

The detective said, "We need to do some surveillance on him. You are right he may have several women he's seeing at one time. But I will be the one following him. Not you. That isn't safe."

Terry asked, "Can I do a ride along with you? I might be of assistance. I sure would like to see his face when he is arrested."

Paul said, "I can arrange a ride-along. But you will have to do exactly as I say."

It was arranged for Paul to pick her up at 7 a.m., and they would go to the house where Arnold was last seen.

At 7:30 they watched Arnold come out, kiss a younger woman goodbye then drive off. The younger woman fit the bank's description of the woman who had opened her safe deposit box.

Detective Leland had several years of experience tracking criminals. They followed Arnold Akers to Mom's Café, where he met another woman. He greeted her with a kiss, and they sat at a booth. After breakfast she got into a silver Lexus, and Paul got her license plate info as she drove out of the lot. They followed Arnold to the Mayfield Street address, where he picked up the woman from yesterday. They followed them to Barnes and Noble Book Store.

Paul told Terry about the woman after Arnold picked her up. "The woman he picked up is Joy Lawson, a widow, 43 years old. She owns her home and a couple of rental properties."

Paul placed a call to his partner to meet him at Barnes and Noble, and asked for a search on the woman in the Lexus. He was told that the search warrants he requested for the two houses had been issued.

Detective Paul Leland and his partner Marcus Stevens made the arrest as Arnold Akers and Joy Lawson came out of the bookstore.

Detective Leland spoke on his radio and then said, "Terry, officers have already picked up the younger woman and are enacting a search warrant for the house, vehicles, and bank accounts. You did well tracking him and the girlfriend, too. The woman he was with now, Joy Lawson met him about a week ago. She is grateful you tracked him down so she didn't get robbed. She said to tell you thanks for saving her from a con man."

He added. "I wouldn't want you mad and taking revenge on me."

Terry said, "Thanks Paul. Arnold in jail and my emeralds back will be sweet revenge."

Detective Paul Leland said, "I'll let you know when I finish the book and maybe we could go out for dinner and discuss your famous great-great grandmother's adventure. Is that okay with you?"

Terry James said, "I'd love that. Maybe spying on people is in my family DNA."

CONETTA TAYLOR, RSCP

Conetta not only loves to write, but she's an avid reader as well. She has stories published in numerous anthologies and is working on other publications. Currently she is editing her debut novel for 2024.

A member of several local writing groups, Conetta loves to attend the educational meetings of each group, writers' conferences and workshops.

Happily-ever-after married for over forty years. Husband, Thom and she live in the beautiful Ozarks. She enjoys a good cup of tea, art and antiques, fun with friends, is faith based and looks for the good in life.

The story she submitted for this publication was written based on a 3-word prompt from her critique group.

Enjoy!

THE HOUSE AT WICKED THICKET

"Edie, come over right away. I got a letter in the mail that you simply won't believe. Hurry! I'm brewing tea."

Edith Gross looked at her husband as he put groceries away. "That was Mercy. What on earth can that be about?" she asked.

"Who knows, but you better go find out before she comes over here. You know she can talk a person to death. At least if you go there, you can leave her house easier than getting her to leave ours."

"You're right. I'll be back."

Edith was still parking in Mercy's driveway when her friend came out the door waving a sheet of paper. "What?" Edith asked on her way to the porch.

"Do you remember me telling you I entered a contest to win a house?"

Well, that was a trick question. Mercy was always talking, and it was easy to not hear everything she said. Plus, her favorite pastime was entering contests. So, no she didn't remember. "Which contest was that?"

They went inside and sat at the table. Tea and cookies served, Edie prompted her to continue. "Mercy, what is this all about?"

"I won a house." She smiled.

"What house?"

"On September Lake in Arkansas. It's called the Mercurial House on Eerie Road."

"How did you win it?"

"One of those contests where they allow up to 10,000 people to write a letter, up to 300 words, explaining why they would like to own that house. Everyone pays a $100 entry fee. The owners read all the letters and pick one to be the next owner. I won!"

"Oh my gosh, Mercy. Tell me about the house. When do you get it?"

"I just talked to them for three hours. We can do title transfer on the first of next month. I can move in any time after that.

"Have you even been to Arkansas?"

"No. Sight unseen. It's out in the country on the lake. She said it's four miles down Eerie Road, a creek gravel road. But look, here's a picture of it."

"That's a huge Victorian." Edith wasn't sure how to respond. "Mercy, does it have any ramps to get inside? It'd be difficult for you to climb those steps."

"I don't care. How much can a ramp cost anyway? I'll be fine."

"What about reaching all those floors? All those staircases?"

"It has an elevator."

"Does it say anything about the condition of the house? Maintenance costs can be pretty scary."

"Relax, Edith. They said it's in good repair. That's all I need."

"Sure, okay. I'm just thinking, eight miles of gravel road every time you go anywhere could be rough on car tires."

"If it was really bad, they wouldn't use rocks. It'll be fine." Mercy sighed. "I'm so excited! She said I can go down anytime next week to see it. Will you and David come with me?"

"Sure. But that's a long way from Peoria. You know David, he'll want to drive."

Mercy waved her hand. "That's fine, I'm too excited to drive myself anyway." She refreshed their tea.

"Have you thought about what you might do with such a huge house in the middle of nowhere? Maybe a bed and breakfast. It'll help pay for its upkeep that way."

"It did cross my mind to do that."

"Furnishing it will cost a lot. Especially if you want furniture true to the era."

"It comes furnished. Most of it is original to when the house was built. They don't want to split it up."

"When was that?"

"Eighteen-ninety-four."

"Wow. It's been around a while."

"I know! Older than me." Mercy jumped up and went to the refrigerator then returned with a couple slices of homemade apple pie.

"Are there other houses down that road?"

"Doesn't sound like it. There are several rental fishing cabins around the lake, though. I wonder if my name helped me win it. The Mercurial House. On Eerie Road and all."

"Do you get any land with it?"

"There's a five-acre clearing around the house. Otherwise, the wooded area around it is called The Wicked Thicket. Isn't that intriguing?"

"Mercy, have you really thought about this? It sounds deserted down Eerie Road. The woods are called the Wicked Thicket. The house is called the Mercurial House, all on September Lake. Have you considered the house might be haunted?"

"Oh, it is! In the top ten most haunted houses in America. Well, you know I hate being alone. This way I'll always have someone to talk to."

NANCY B. DAILEY

Nancy Dailey is a former Missouri schoolteacher who has traveled across the United States, Germany, the Netherlands and took a solo trip to Suriname to do research for her books. Her artwork has been exhibited in multiple countries, and she's won several awards for her miniature portraits. A longtime member of Sleuths' Ink, Nancy has served as President, Vice President, Secretary and Treasurer. Never one to shy away from adventure, she took up zip lining for her 70th birthday and was in excellent health until ALS appeared. Her published books include *Chasing Caterpillars: The Life and Times of Maria Sybilla Merian, Jim the Wonder Dog and Knadel's Ghost.*

Rest in Peace, friend.

WAYPOINT MURDER

He ran, slowly now, breathing in ragged gasps. He stumbled on a tree root and fell. Jack Hughes had been geocaching, following his GPS, trying to locate the "Bum Cache". He had made it to within thirty feet of the cache.

Jack had gone online that morning to see if there were any new caches listed near his hometown in southwest Missouri. There were three. He had entered the coordinates into his GPS, along with the cache names, before leaving home and heading into the woods on the north side of town.

Geocaching was a new hobby for Jack. It was like a modern-day treasure hunt, but the value of the "treasures" was minimal. For Jack, finding the caches was the main thing. But he did carry small items with him to trade. That was the rule: take something, leave something.

He'd had no idea when he left home that less than an hour later, he'd be running for his life.

A twig snapped. Jack looked for cover. There, ahead, was a lot of brush. He got up, staggered a few steps, and fell into the undergrowth.

As his breathing quieted, Jack thought about what he had seen. At first, he thought it was another geocacher, and he stayed back to let him make the find. But the guy, dressed in dirty overalls, was using a shovel. Caches were to be hidden but not buried. Then he noticed the long, lumpy, dirty blue sheet tied at both ends. Was that a person wrapped in that sheet? A dead person? I've been watching too many movies, Jack thought. But then the guy tossed the shovel aside, bent down and rolled the lumpy sheet into...a grave?

Jack stepped back; the movement caught the guy's eye. He looked straight at Jack for a full second, then calmly reached for the double-curved bow leaning against a nearby tree. He chose an arrow from the quiver, then slung the quiver over his shoulder.

"Yer trespassin', son. Ya know what I do to trespassers?" he growled. He fitted the shaft of the arrow against the bowstring. Jack ran.

Now he carefully raised his head to look around. He heard the arrow as it whizzed past. He didn't wait to see where it went; he ran, crouched, on a zig-zag course from behind one tree to another. Suddenly he was sliding down into a ravine. He heard laughter from somewhere above.

Frantically he looked around. There was a large outcrop of rocks on his left, with a thick stand of cedar trees on the other side. Jack scrabbled his way around the rocks and pushed his way into the cedars. He held his breath, listening.

Facing the gully, he could see a large patch of sunshine at the edge of the trees. He slid the GPS along the ground into the sunshine, pushing buttons until he was back on the page for the "Bum Cache". He changed the name. He then checked the location of his car, thankful that he had actually marked it. The arrow pointed across the gully.

Jack dashed across the bottom of the gully and into the trees on the other side. He reached the top of the embankment without further incident. There was the gravel road; he saw his car parked about fifty yards away.

Just as he reached for the door, a voice behind him

boomed. "Goin' somewhere, sonny?"

Jack whirled around. Less than twenty feet away stood the guy with the bow and arrow.

"Naw, you ain't goin' nowhere." The guy grinned.

They both heard the sound of tires on gravel and glanced toward the noise. The guy in the overalls quickly lowered his bow. The County Sheriff's car appeared around the curve, slowed then stopped.

The sheriff got out and walked over.

"Mornin', Clint," said the guy with the bow and arrows.

"Mornin', Bud," replied the sheriff. "You boys seen Miz Lucy's Doberman? He's loose again."

"Naw," said Bud. Jack shook his head.

"Been huntin' this mornin'?" asked the sheriff, eyeing Bud's bow and arrow.

"Jest some rabbit," Bud replied.

"No, Sheriff, that's not true!" countered Jack. "This man's trying to kill me."

"That right, Bud?" asked the sheriff.

"Naw, this feller got hisself lost and I was jest tryin' to help him outta the woods. Scared him, mebbe, tha's all."

"Sheriff, I saw him dump what looked like a body wrapped in a sheet into a shallow grave he'd just dug. Then he saw me and came after me."

"Aw, this feller's got a big imagination," drawled Bud. "It wuz a big load a garbage I wuz getting' rid of."

The sheriff nodded. "How's the wife, Bud?"

"She's off visitin' her aunt in St. Louis again. Don't know why anybody in their right mind'd wanna go there."

"I heard she came back last week," said the sheriff. "Miz Jones said she saw her get off the bus in town Wednesday afternoon."

"Yeah, well she got some more clothes and went back," said Bud.

"Isn't that rather strange for her to just go right back?" asked the sheriff.

Bud shrugged his shoulders.

"That might be his wife he buried," suggested Jack.

"You cain't pin nuthin' on me," growled Bud.

The sheriff looked at Jack. "What were you doin' in the woods, anyway?" he asked.

"I was geocaching, looking for a hidden cache, using my GPS to help me find it when I saw this guy. He dumped the body, then saw me and came after me with his bow and arrows."

Jack handed the GPS to the sheriff. "Check this, it will lead you to the body."

"Looks like I'm gonna have to take you in, Bud," said the sheriff as he pulled out his handcuffs.

"I didn't do nuthin'," protested Bud.

"You ain't got nuthin' on me."

"Better get in the car, Bud." The sheriff radioed for backup. Then he turned to Jack.

"Geocaching's usually a pretty fun sport," he said, taking Jack's GPS. "I like to do it some, too." He quickly went to the waypoints page. "Which one, son?"

"You'll find it under Waypoint Murder," said Jack.

Originally published in Caching Now, October, 2009.

UNSCHEDULED TRAIN STOP

Christine and I, both 18 that spring of 1959, boarded the train in Athens for our return trip to Germany. Our vacation in Greece had been cut short when her aunt, our chaperone, unexpectedly died—but that's another story.

We found seats in a third-class compartment, hoisted our luggage onto the overhead racks, and settled in. Yugoslavia was the first place I had ever seen military uniforms on train personnel. It was intimidating to say the least.

A whistle blew. A jerk signaled the wheels beginning to turn, and in no time we rolled noisily through the Greek countryside, stopping all too soon at the Yugoslavian border.

Once again, we had papers to fill out before entering that country. Once again, I had to write down the amount of money I had with me. Once again, I had to list exactly how many coins and bills of each denomination in the currencies that I had—German Marks and Greek drachmas. Since we would not be allowed to step off the train anywhere in Yugoslavia, and there was nothing on board to purchase, not even food, this seemed absolutely ridiculous.

We handed our paperwork to the scowling, uniformed Yugoslavian officials who boarded the train. They also asked to see our passports, visas, and tickets. Check, check, check. This began the constant harassment, day and night, at regular intervals. First came the "Uniform" demanding to see our passports. Next came a second "Uniform" to check our visas. Then came a third "Uniform" to look at our tickets. Over and over again.

Unlike the previous trip, the passengers in our compartment seemed disinclined to talk. I couldn't help but compare the murmur of various languages previously with the total silence now. A memory made me smile. I had sat by the window. A young soldier sat by the door across from me. He wanted to talk. The conversation became international, with everyone involved translating from one language to another to another, and finally Christine, sitting next to me, made the final translation into English. My replies made the return trip translations back to the soldier.

At some point the soldier said that he would get off the train at the last stop before the border and that he would be escorted off. He had special permission to visit his sick parents who lived very close to the border, and the military was making sure that he did not take the opportunity to leave the country. Sure enough, at the designated time, an armed officer came for him. Trying to wrap my mind around such a situation, I felt incredible sadness for the young soldier. And I realized how much of my own culture was based on trust in one another.

Lulled by the motion of the train, I stared out the window at the people working in the fields without modern machinery, using simple hand tools. They reminded me of paintings I had seen in museums. Christine tried out the languages she knew and found a young man to visit with.

The train stopped. In the middle of nowhere. The same thing had happened two or three times on our way to Greece. We never knew why. After a while the train moved on.

Around noon people brought out food they had packed

for the trip, even sharp knives for cutting slices of meat. Delicious smells filled the compartment. Christine and I had not thought this out as well as the other passengers. We had only bread, cheese, and fruit. No cutlery.

Late in the afternoon the train made another unscheduled stop. The compartment door slammed open and a "Uniform" pointed to the luggage overhead and motioned everybody out. I had no clue what he said. We dutifully grabbed our luggage and carried it with us, trudging down the aisle past other compartments to the end of the train car, down the steps off the train. What? Off the train?!

We stood there in the sunshine and fresh air looking around at each other. Nobody said anything. Then some people started walking alongside the train away from the engine. We followed. Had they discovered something wrong with our car? Was that why we were being moved?

At the top step I discovered why the transfer was taking so long. A mountain of luggage piled in the aisle obscured a good part of the windows. Some people sat atop piled suitcases, others stood in what was left of the aisle, leaning against the compartments. We had to climb over suitcases, odd shaped packages, canvas sacks, and one brightly woven bag with a live chicken whose head stuck out of the tied top, all the while lifting our own stuff up and over. We worked our way to a less crowded spot. All of the third-class compartments were filled with extra people sitting on their luggage on the floor between the two facing bench seats. We hefted our bags on top of others in the aisle and stood there.

Suddenly the train jerked as the wheels began rolling, and those of us standing did a quick two-step to maintain our balance.

This was going to be a long trip.

Christine, bored, said she was going to talk with some other people. Off she went plowing through, climbing over, making her way towards a cluster of people near the stairs. I stayed put.

When she returned, she grabbed her suitcase and said, "C'mon, Nancy. I got permission for us to sit in first class."

I did not doubt that at all. She was a tall, natural blonde with a winning smile, and eyes that drew you in.

It felt good to sit down again! The seats were more comfortable than in third class and had leg room! I relaxed.

The same three "Uniforms" continued their routine. Nothing was said about the tickets.

Christine went back to her newfound friends. I pulled out a book to read. The "Uniforms" came through again.

The next time when the "Uniform" asked to see my passport, I handed it to him, he looked at it and handed it back. I went back to reading. A quiet little thought said that was not the same passport guy. I brushed the thought aside.

The next "Uniform" asked for my visa. That's not the same visa guy. I shrugged the thought aside.

The ticket "Uniform" asked for my ticket. I handed it to him, waiting for him to hand it back. Instead he grew about two inches, a dark scowl appeared on his face, and he yelled at me. I had no idea what he said, but I knew for certain that he was MAD. When I didn't say anything he raged some more. If smoke could have come out of his ears, I'm sure it would have. He thrust his hand towards me, angrily shouting, "Pass! Pass!" That I understood. I handed him my passport.

He abruptly turned and left. With my passport!

I needed my passport!

I sat alone in the compartment, shaking.

How far is the border? How many days would it take to walk there? No passport; I'll have to sneak into Austria. I visualized myself on high alert, treading quietly through a forest, crossing an invisible border and emerging into Austria and freedom. There I could speak and understand enough to explain the situation.

The video in my head came to a screeching halt when the compartment door slid open and two men entered. One was the ticket guy, the other an unassuming little man who kept ducking his head as he talked. It took a minute before I realized he was struggling to speak some form of English. It took even longer for me to understand. I would be taken off the train at the next stop.

The little man had barely left when the train slowed down. I felt the tentacles of panic relentlessly twisting their way inside me.

As the train came to a complete stop, two huge muscular men entered, one on each side of me. They each grabbed one of my forearms and hoisted me up, out, and down the steps onto the station platform. To be truthful, they walked. I did not. They held me so tightly and so high that, although my feet were moving, they did not touch the ground. I felt like I was in a Saturday morning TV kids cartoon, but it wasn't funny.

Two other men had escorted a middle eastern man in a business suit off the train also. He had dark hair, well cut, and a nice looking mustache. While the four men conferred, Mr. Mustachio spoke to me. I did not understand. He tried a different language. Again I could not respond. Then he spoke German. He must have seen a flash of understanding in my eyes, for he began a conversation. Had I been in a first class compartment while holding a third class ticket? he asked. I nodded. He said they crowded people into cars like this to make money, but all I had to do was spend a night in jail and they would let me go.

Jail?! My face must have registered sheer terror.

He quickly told me not to say anything, he would take care of everything. I had no trouble not speaking; I felt paralyzed.

We were ushered into an office at the train station. Our passports were given to a man in uniform, who handed them to someone else who promptly disappeared into another room. I know Mr. Mustachio talked with this uniformed man in charge because I saw their mouths moving. Nothing else registered.

Mr. Mustachio pulled out his wallet and counted out several bills, handing them over. The next thing I remember is seeing a man come out of a back room with our passports. My eyes zoomed in on my passport and stayed there. I watched as they were handed to the main official behind the desk. He stood up, holding them but not moving them in our direction. I felt antsy.

It seemed like an hour before he held my passport out towards me. I snatched it and held it close. Mr. Mustachio took my arm and we quickly left the office—just in time to see the train pick up speed as it left the station! The official deliberately held onto our passports to make sure the train left without us.

My mind went blank. Yes, it IS possible to have absolutely nothing in, on, or possibly even under your mind. Nothing at all. Nothing.

Mr. Mustachio pulled me along with him, saying, "Run!" I ran. We ran around to the front of the station, got into an ancient looking black car, and took off. Still no thoughts. But I did register what I saw. The car looked like those I'd seen in old black and white films. I was aware that we sped down a super highway devoid of cars. We did pass a couple of wooden wagons, both pulled by…cows?

The driver stomped on the brake and held it down. We kept going. Gradually we slowed, careened onto a one lane dirt road. Nothing in sight. The driver's foot was still on the brake pedal. We rounded a curve, and I spied a small train station ahead. The car finally stopped right in front of it.

We got out. I watched Mr. Mustachio and the driver go into the station. My brain slowly began working again. Of course they both went in. To get a receipt to account for the missing money when we got to the border.

I saw a train in the distance, getting closer. I wonder

where this train goes?

Mr. Mustachio joined me shortly before the train pulled in and came to a stop. He guided me to a car to get on. As I reached the top step I saw a mountain of luggage, packages, and people.

I heard an angry, "Nancy!"

There stood Christine, scowling.

"WHERE HAVE YOU BEEN?!"

I was speechless. I was back on the same car, the same train I had been kicked off of!

I never saw that nameless middle eastern gentleman again. He has no idea what an impact he made on my life, but because of him, every person I meet has my respect until they prove otherwise. I have had the privilege and enjoyment of knowing many people from a variety of places and circumstances, all of whom have greatly enriched my life. Thank you, Mr. Mustachio, whoever you are. I have never forgotten what you did for me that day and beyond.

OTHER BOOKS BY CONTRIBUTORS

Find other books by the some anthology contributors at Amazon, Barnes & Noble, BAM and other online retailers.

R.H. Burkett – https://tinyurl.com/rhburkett
DeDe Ramey – https://tinyurl.com/dederamey
Shirley McCann – https://tinyurl.com/shirleymccann
James R. Wilder – https://tinyurl.com/jamesrwilder
Margarite Stever – https://tinyurl.com/margaritestever
J.C. Fields – https://tinyurl.com/jcfields
Ken Gardner – https://tinyurl.com/kengardner
Sharon Kizziah-Holmes – https://tinyurl.com/skholmes
VJ Schultz – https://tinyurl.com/vjschultz
Lois Curran – https://tinyurl.com/loiscurran
Duane Laflin – https://tinyurl.com/duanelaflin
Drew Thorn – https://tinyurl.com/drewthorn
Sage Hunter – https://tinyurl.com/sagehunter
Rosalie Lombardo – https://tinyurl.com/rosalielombardo
Janet Kay Gallagher – https://tinyurl.com/jangallagher

Made in the USA
Coppell, TX
17 September 2023

21655825R00152